BY LONNIE BUSCH

Without a Face
Assimilation
The Anything Room
Cargo Hold 4
All Hope of Becoming Human
The Baldwin Hotel
The Cabin on Souder Hill
Push Me:Feisty Stories of Love & Loss
Turnback Creek; a Novella & Six Stories

WITHOUT A FACE

LONNIE BUSCH

Human Authored Reg #: 6616898, https://authorsguild.org/human

UBiQ PRESS

No AI was used for any part of this book

WITHOUT A FACE

A UBiQ PRESS BOOK

North Carolina, USA

https://lonniebusch.com/

Cover Art by Lonnie Busch

ISBN: 978-1-964024-17-2 (hardcover)

ISBN: 978-1-964024-16-5 (paperback)

First Paperback/Hardcover Editions, March 2026

Library of Congress Control Number: 2026908448

Human Authored Reg #: 6616898, https://authorsguild.org/human

WITHOUT
A
FACE

Chapter One

W*e interrupt this program to bring you this Special News Bulletin.*

Kurt looked up from his newspaper. Alice was gone from the living room, steam rising from her cup of tea on the coffee table.

Walter Cronkite filled the television screen, his expression grave and focused, but the volume was too low to understand what he was saying. Displayed in white letters on the black lower-third bar below the iconic newscaster were just two words: Deadly Virus.

"Alice?" Kurt called from his lounger, levering the chair back to its upright position, the footrest folding in underneath. Alice appeared in the wide opening between the living room and kitchen, the olive-colored phone pressed to her ear. The coiled cord was stretched tight as she mouthed the word, *Sally,* pointing at the receiver.

Kurt nodded and got up as Alice swept back into the kitchen, as if the taut phone cord had reeled her back in. He reached down and twisted the volume knob on their Magnavox set until the deep resonance of Mr. Cronkite's voice rang through clearly.

"The Communicable Disease Center is warning all Americans to get vaccinated," the trusted anchor said. "We will update you as more information becomes available."

Now back to your regularly scheduled program.

When the program resumed, the screen showed three futuristic spacecraft battling in outer space, laser streaks whistling between the combatants, strikes landing with loud explosions. Kurt expected the scene was far more dramatic in color, but he and Alice had opted to keep their black and white set. The scene cut away to Mr. Spock pleading with Captain Kirk, while the crew at their stations frantically worked to get the skirmish under control. It was a relatively new show, and they'd watched a few episodes the previous fall, but Kurt didn't much care for it. When he pushed the knob to turn off the set the screen fell dark.

He went back to his chair and had just picked up his newspaper when Alice returned to the living room. She glanced at the dark set.

"I thought we were going to watch Gomer Pyle?" she said, bringing her cup of tea to her lips.

"*Star Trek* is on," he said into his newspaper. Kurt was reading an article about the NASA launch of Surveyor 3 which took place only a few days ago. The probe was tasked with analyzing lunar soil for a potential moon landing sometime in the future. The article also revisited the horrific cabin fire aboard Apollo 1 three months earlier, on January 27, 1967, at Cape Kennedy. The fire, which occurred during a launch rehearsal test, killed all three crew members—Command Pilot Gus Grissom, Senior Pilot Ed White, and Pilot Roger B. Chaffee.

According to the article, all crewed Apollo flights were suspended while the fire was under investigation, though testing of the lunar module and Saturn V rocket continued. Kurt was about to tell Alice about the Surveyor 3 lunar probe headed to the moon when she turned the TV set back on.

Once the picture came up, she rotated the channel selector until she found *Gomer Pyle, U.S.M.C.* The reception was bad, so she fiddled with the rabbit ears, shifting each antenna back and forth until the picture cleared, eliminating the horizontal snow. She smiled, backing up to her chair to sit down. About to sip her cup of tea, she said, "Jim Nabors has such a beautiful voice. You wouldn't know it to look at him with that goofy grin."

Kurt could only nod, as he had never liked that show much, either, and had never actually heard Jim Nabors sing. But he trusted his wife's assessment, as she too had a beautiful voice though used it so seldom it seemed a shame.

"Sally was telling me about a virus sweeping the country," Alice said when Gomer Pyle show went to commercials.

"Yeah, I just saw a Special News Bulletin. Walter Cronkite was talking about it."

"Oh, I like him…. What did he have to say?"

"I just caught the tail end of it."

"Sally was saying folks are supposed to get vaccinated, but she isn't going to. She said we all live so far out in the sticks that a virus would need a Rand McNally roadmap to find us!"

Kurt chuckled, though didn't much care for Sally either. He'd only met her a few times, but it only took once to realize she was a gossipy beautician with a grating voice and a bigger-than-life imagination, going on about conspiracy theories and UFOs.

"Sally and Duncan are headed over to the Sizzler tomorrow night," Alice said. "They invited us to go with them."

A big steak and baked potato sounded great, if only he

didn't have to endure Sally's fantastic yarns and Duncan's stories about the feed business. But Kurt could endure just about anything if a big juicy steak was in the offing.

They had planned to stay home all weekend, but met the couple for dinner anyway. Kurt sliced his steak into hearty chunks while Sally talked about folks over in Destine and Downfall who'd mysteriously gone missing. "They drove off one day and never returned," Sally said. "People came into the shop talking about it."

Kurt ignored her. He hadn't seen anything in the newspaper, or heard a thing on the TV about missing residents. Another of her fantastical ramblings, Kurt figured. Alice took his hand beneath the table, as if to thank him for enduring Sally's gossipy rants.

"Some just vanished from their homes during the night!" Sally added, her husband sitting quietly next to her, working his fork inside his baked potato slathered with butter and sour cream. "Car still sitting in the driveway in the morning!" Sally added, sitting back in the booth, her arm bent at the elbow, her fingers near her chin scissoring a Virginia Slim.

"Can you imagine that?" she added, a thin ribbon of smoke escaping the corner of her mouth like a genie.

Kurt *couldn't* imagine it, and was just about to tell her so, when Alice squeezed his hand and smiled over at him.

Once they finished dinner, Kurt was glad to get in the Rambler and head for home. He and Alice didn't talk much in the car until Alice asked if he was perplexed by Sally. Kurt told her he was glad they had gotten out of the house, that visiting with the couple hadn't been as bad as he'd expected it to be.

"You're such a handsome liar," Alice said, placing her hand on his thigh.

"I didn't say it *wasn't* bad…just not as bad as I thought it would be."

On Sunday they went to the cemetery to visit Reed's grave. It had been five years since they'd lost their son. Kurt could still picture the overturned tractor in the culvert, could still remember how his chest hollowed out running toward his son, assuring himself that Reed would have jumped free before it crushed him.

The fiction didn't hold. The three of them were all crushed that day; Reed beneath the tractor, Kurt and Alice beneath the devastating death of their only child. The memory had faded somewhat, but still had the power to stop his breath.

Alice brought flowers for the grave, while Kurt picked the dried leaves and dead sticks off the grass. They sat quietly with their son, until Alice said she was getting hungry. Kurt was too, and suggested they stop at McDonald's on the way home. Alice preferred to heat up the stew she'd made a few nights earlier.

That evening, they ate their dinner in the living room on TV trays, watching television, then read their books in bed before they readied for sleep.

"Do you want to open the window tonight, Kurt?" Alice said, sitting up in her nightgown in the dark. "There's a nice breeze."

Kurt got out of bed and walked to the window, pushing it up until the curtains swayed. He sighed, looking down at the dark driveway, shadows from the security lamp stretching across the gravel, recalling the cemetery, the clouds passing above Reed's headstone, the coolness riding the late afternoon air, then sitting with Alice in the living room watching television, his mind suddenly shifting to the unsettling topics Sally had talked about at the Sizzler the previous evening. The story about the missing people lingered in the back of his thoughts. It wasn't the subject matter that bothered him so much as Sally's unwavering conviction that the stories were true.

"Are you all right, Kurt?"

Alice's words drifted lovingly to his ears. It was always like music to him, her voice, whether she was singing in the shower, or asking him to take out the trash.

"I'm perfect," he said smiling over at her. "With you in my life, everything's perfect."

CHAPTER TWO

Disoriented, Kurt pushed up on one elbow trying to call back the sound that woke him. The bedroom was dark, the curtains shifting like wraiths from the breeze slipping through the open window. He glanced at Alice, wrapped in blankets next to him, sleeping like a mummy. A second later his groggy mind came to attention. The noise filling the background of his dreams turned out to be the low grumble of an idling car engine. It sounded as if it issued from the open window, rising up from the driveway to the second story of their home.

Kurt quietly cleared his throat and eased the covers off, letting his feet drift soundlessly toward the floor. The hands on the alarm clock read 3:42. The box springs screeched gently as he lifted his weight from the mattress. Sneaking a quick look over his shoulder to see if Alice stirred, he stretched his back a moment, listening. Time was trapped in a dusky, unmoving torpor. Even the curtains had stopped breathing.

Kurt took his first step toward the window, the sole of his foot sucking down to the bare varnished plank floor.

Squeak, squeak, squeak, the old boards complained. The low growl of moving metal parts outside kept monotonous vigil over his trek across the bedroom. He suppressed a sniffle, his sinuses beginning to open, the smell of exhaust squeezing out the sweet fragrance of Alice's ceramic bowl filled with dried petals and spices.

The volume of the thrumming engine increased perfectly in sync with Kurt's proximity to the window, until it nearly sounded as if the machinery were in the room with him. It was no longer something out there, but something in here. Close. Out of place. Their house sat at least a quarter-mile from the main road which serviced very little traffic. It didn't even have a real name, just Route N. Images rolled through Kurt's imagination as to what he would see when he sent his eyes to the sound below.

The driveway appeared gauzy, dark and unformed, filled with contradicting shadows and indistinguishable puddles of dull light, the terrain difficult to parse. Slowly, the image of a dark car roof separated itself from the shadows of trees and shrubs. At first glance it appeared to be the black hearse from Gorten Funeral Home. Old Man Gorten's official car. Then Kurt noticed it was a sedan.

The taillights spilled out weak red light, exhaust swirling in the crimson glow. Kurt let his attention trace a path toward the windshield, his eyes trying to dig into the blackness of the front seat. It was impenetrable. At the front end of the sedan was a shape. Kurt was having difficulty with it. The glare from the headlights made it nearly impossible to puzzle out. Until it moved. A man, he thought, in a dark overcoat and trousers...and wearing a fedora?

Apparently, the stranger had his eyes downcast, his legs crossed at the ankles, his body propped against the front fender covering the driver's side headlamp. The top of the stranger's black fedora hid his face. Even so, it certainly wasn't old man Gorten or anyone else Kurt knew from town.

Just then, Kurt spied a tiny orange light that glowed like a fiery ember before subsiding. A second later a thin snake of smoke slithered out from beneath his hat. The acrid stink of nicotine reached the upstairs window. The man took one last drag, then flipped the butt toward the grassy edge of the driveway. Kurt was frozen, unable to move, unable to ask the stranger what he was up to.

Alice stirred across the room, shifting Kurt's attention for just a moment. When he brought his eyes back to the driveway, the stranger had his head cocked back, looking up at him, though Kurt was still unable to see his features. Kurt stumbled back from the window, his heart racing, checking Alice first, then his shotgun in the corner. Maybe he should go down and phone the sheriff…*load the shotgun first!*

The gun had been propped in the corner for months, ever since he told Alice he was going grouse hunting. He never went, though. That was last fall, and it seemed every day since Alice begged him to put the gun back in the garage. He thought maybe hauling it out into the woods might bring back the memory of when he took Reed hunting. They only went once, and it had been a horrible outing. Reed's feet were freezing in the early winter snow, and he became horribly distressed by the awful racket. And when they walked over to the grouse Kurt had shot, the boy had to turn away. He was only nine, and wanted no part of it. They never went again. What had Kurt been thinking, wanting to relive that day?

He hurried across the room, trying not to startle Alice. When he reached for the weapon, his fingers missed, sending it sliding down the wall and clattering across the hardwood floor.

"Kurt? What was that?" Alice said, poking her head up from the covers. "What are you doing?"

"Go back to sleep, Alice," Kurt said, fumbling to pick up the gun while keeping it hidden from her.

"What are you doing with the shotgun?" Now she was sitting up, her nightgown hanging off her thin shoulders, her head shifting in the dark.

"Just go to sleep." Kurt cracked the shotgun open, checking for shells. One. Maybe that was enough. He hadn't fired the damn thing in so long the shell might not even be good. He scrambled to the dresser, gently easing the top drawer open to keep from upsetting the framed picture of his son. The picture sat there every day for years, but in this odd light, it seemed that Reed—only nine when that picture was taken, smiling up from the small plastic pool in the backyard—was squinting, and Kurt couldn't see his eyes. He had never realized that before, and it made the boy's face seem pressed with worry, or fear.

Kurt looked away, scrubbing his hand through the drawer, his fingers shuffling past his folded boxer shorts to find the container of shells.

"Kurt! You're scaring me!" Alice threw the covers back, launching from the bed. She was halfway across the room when her attention snagged on the open window. Maybe she heard the engine, or smelled cigarette smoke. She eased closer. "Who's that man in our driveway?"

Kurt found the box and withdrew two fresh shells, then jerked the old one from the gun before jamming the fresh ones into the chamber. After snapping the barrel shut, he hurried toward the window.

"What are you gonna do, Kurt?" Alice's face shone pale, like a ghastly mask, her spindly arms lashed rope-like across her chest. She looked so frail, Kurt thought, edging her away from the window.

"Get back, Alice." She eased away, staying within arms-reach of him.

When Kurt looked down at the driveway, his breath caught. The sedan was still idling, the engine running, but the man was gone. Just then they heard the front screen door screech open and slam shut. The intruder wasn't bothering to conceal his entrance.

Kurt rushed from the window and swung the bedroom door closed, quickly locking it. He directed Alice toward the corner of the room, waving her away with his free hand. She moved with hesitation, frightened, like a confused mouse, shifting her gaze between the dark corner and Kurt, pleading with her eyes to let her stay close to him, as if there were greater safety in numbers. But he couldn't have it. He shooed her away with an impatient scowl, gesturing to keep moving away, forcing her into the far corner until she was wedged so tightly, she couldn't move. There she stood, trembling, her eyes wide, her mouth twisted with fear, tears dripping down her nightgown.

Kurt swallowed, his mouth like sandpaper, a frenetic fear coursing through him. Is that what it was? Fear? He couldn't recall a time he'd been this scared. After Reed was killed in the tractor accident, Kurt and Alice led a quiet life. Just the two of them, keeping their garden, tending the cows, planting a few of the fields and keeping to themselves. They hardly went into town other than to shop for groceries, or to get his '56 Nash Rambler serviced. Reed, their son, used to tease him about their cream-colored Nash when he was in high school, telling him they should get something newer, cooler. "Look at this convertible!" Reed had told him, the slick magazine page crinkling under his excitement. It was the latest model at the time, a 1961 Chevy Impala, fire-engine red. But to Kurt it was an unreasonable choice. With routine oil changes and tire rotation, the Nash ran just fine. Reed never admitted as much, but Kurt knew his son was embarrassed to ask girls out on dates because of their frumpish automobile. A year later Reed was dead, and frugality never seemed important after that.

Footfalls coming down the hallway jolted Kurt from the memory. A moment later a knock came at the door. Kurt's heart pounded like a piston. Alice slumped to the floor, her knees pulled to her chin, her body wound into a tight ball. The sight broke Kurt's heart; it was exactly how she looked when he gave her the news about Reed.

"Mister!" Kurt screamed at the locked door. "I don't know what you're doing in my house, but you need to turn right around and walk yourself out to that automobile and be on your way."

Kurt waited, shooting glances Alice's way, then back to the door. Alice was sobbing audibly now, convulsing, mewling in the dark corner.

"I'm not playing, mister. Go on. Get!" Kurt was tearing up, heat rising in his chest, and was glad Alice couldn't see his face in the darkened bedroom. As a hale young man, he'd never shied from a fight or argument, and at just over six-three and nearly 240 pounds of muscle, not many would've tried him in this region, much less in their little town of Rescue. But that was an earlier version of Kurt Franklin, before sleep apnea, gout, and blood thinners. Before his weight dropped to 210 pounds. Now he was forever saddled wearing bib overalls, or had to lash his belts so tight his trousers bunched up in the back.

The door knob rattled and Kurt didn't know if he could backup his threat. Maybe the intruder needed more information to sway his thinking, but was Kurt willing to kill a man? Twenty years ago, it wouldn't have been a question…the man would be lying dead on the linoleum floor. Kurt wanted to believe he was a more courageous man in his younger days, but wasn't sure if that assumption really held up. It had never been tested. Not like this.

Kurt took a deep breath. "That's it, mister! I got me a double-barreled twelve-gauge pointed at the door, and if I don't hear that sedan of yours pulling from my driveway in the next few minutes, you and me are gonna have a problem!"

The stranger rapped hard on the wood, like his knuckles were made of steel. Louder and more anxious, the knock came again, until the door handle jiggled erratically, impatiently. An uncomfortable tightness started in Kurt's chest, spreading to his throat. His breathing was labored, his fingertip cold on one of the steel triggers. The knocking at the door sounded irritable and edgy, the knob rattling, the door hardware clattering as if it could fly apart, and Kurt pulled the trigger.

The blast slammed his eardrums, leaving a siren in his skull.

Light from the hallway glowed weakly though the splintered hole, the door ruined, the door knob gone. He pulled the other trigger, the second explosion worse than the first, the smell of gunpowder and smoke filling the room, his legs shuddering in the raw fierceness of the moment. By now Alice was screaming, wailing, covering her head, her face buried in the crux of her crossed arms. Kurt was sure the ringing in his head would never stop, the hole in the door an eerie jagged mouth, bright daggers of wood contrasting years of darkened varnished larch.

Beyond the door Kurt could see nothing of the intruder, not much of anything at all, nothing but an unmoving gloom. He took his eyes to Alice in the far corner, her wailing reduced to a desperate, choking whimper.

Resolve spread through Kurt, a soothing calm knowing he'd done the right thing, protected Alice, their home, their life. A moment later he dropped the shotgun, and went over to his wife, his resolve crumbling, picturing the dead man on the other side of the door. He had every right to kill the man—didn't he? Of course he did. Sheriff Logan would assure him he'd done the right thing.

"Not easy killing a man, Kurt," Sheriff Logan would tell

him when he got to the house, his palm resting on his sidearm. "You did what you had to, Kurt. The law is on your side here."

Kurt squatted down next to Alice and cradled her into his arms. She shook so hard it nearly broke his heart. He pulled her closer, trying to calm her, easing to a sitting position on the floor next to her, squeezing her tighter.

It seemed only moments later—though Kurt had no idea how long it had been—the strangest thing happened.

The bedroom door opened.

Alice didn't move; her body had become still, her eyes aimed at the doorway. Kurt tried to clear his thoughts, twisting his head to follow her gaze. A man stood there, barely visible in the dark doorway. To the shadow beneath his hat, the man brought up a lit cigarette. The tip glowed with the intensity of a fiery planet for just a second before dimming. The foul odor of nicotine drifted over to Kurt, a cloud of smoke leaking out from the silhouette across the room.

"It's time to go, Kurt," the stranger said. "You and Alice need to come with me."

Kurt's heart plunged.

"And before you ask," the intruder said. "You aren't dead…and you're not dreaming."

Kurt hadn't considered either of those two possibilities, though he was confused.

Alice stirred in his arms, holding him tighter. "Kurt?" she whispered. "What's going on? Who is that?"

When they finally saw the intruder's face, Kurt recoiled in horror. Alice swung away from the man so fast into Kurt's chest, he thought she'd broken his ribs. The man's face was ruined from the shotgun blasts—holes and rips in his shirt and suit, even his hat—but no blood, only pocked, shredded flesh and exposed, shiny bone.

The intruder gave them a few minutes to get dressed and grab what they needed. "Only what you can carry," he said, and didn't appear to be in pain. After they'd gotten dressed, and gathered some belongings, the man led them down the hallway of their own home, both of them following like scolded school children headed for the principal's office. The kitchen light was on, which seemed odd, until Kurt noticed the coiled phone cord cut, dangling uselessly from the kitchen handset. Alice had insisted she needed it so she could talk with her friends while she whipped a cake mix, or threw fresh-cut vegetables into a huge pot for stew. And when she found the avocado-colored one that matched the stove and refrigerator, she had to have it.

Passing the kitchen counter, Alice broke away from Kurt and grabbed a butcher knife.

"Alice," the intruder said. "Please put that down."

"Get out of our house, buster!" she said, her hand shaking, her eyes steely as nails. "I'm not kidding!"

Kurt stayed between the man and Alice, hoping to avert disaster. "Go on, mister. You heard her…" Kurt said, unsure how her knife, which looked huge in Alice's small hand, was any threat to someone capable of surviving a double shotgun blast.

Walking to the sink, the man blew out a plume of smoke before dropping his cigarette into the drain. He twisted the water on for just a moment, then walked toward Alice. She swiveled to meet his approach, Kurt stepping closer to present a fortified front.

The man pushed Kurt aside like he was straw, Kurt landing against the kitchen table, losing his balance and ending up on the floor. He was struggling to get up when Alice plunged the knife at the intruder's abdomen, the blade hitting a surface hard enough to knock the weapon free from her grip. It clattered along the floor.

In the brittle silence that followed, the stranger said, "I hope we won't have further incidents."

"He's hurt," Alice said, shaky, touching the blood on Kurt's forehead, her face wrecked with fear.

"He'll be fine," the intruder said. "Let's go."

Kurt assured Alice he was okay.

When they passed through the living room, it felt odd, like a tour of their own possessions, but seen through different eyes. Terrified eyes. Alice clung to Kurt, occasionally fretting with the cut on his forehead, which now hosted a slight bump. Kurt ignored her fussing, his attention focused on everyday objects, now imbued with new meaning, or maybe it was *no* meaning; the newest copy of the TV Guide magazine sitting on the coffee table, William Shatner and Leonard Nimoy of *Star Trek* on the cover.

Against the far wall, sitting on a white crochet lace tablecloth, was the cathedral-shaped wooden Philco radio they'd gotten as a wedding gift from Kurt's parents. Beyond the flowered-couch and Kurt's brown Naugahyde recliner, sat the Magnavox television, its knobs slightly worn, the V-shaped rabbit-ear antennae pointed toward the ceiling.

Kurt walked with numb obedience, following this stranger out the front door, Alice stumbling along with him like a faulty appendage, her whimpering nearly inaudible. Why was he allowing this transgression, this invasion of their freedom? Nevertheless, he felt powerless to rebel, unable to protect her or himself. If the shotgun blasts and the knife hadn't stopped this peculiar man, what could?

The intruder led them to the sedan idling in the driveway. He opened the backdoor on the passenger side and told them to make themselves comfortable in the backseat.

"I'd let one of you sit up front…" the man said as he started to ease the door shut. "But I doubt either of you want to stare at this"—he motioned toward his hideous, ravaged face—"for the next couple hours."

After crossing around to the driver's side, the stranger

folded himself into the front seat, then grabbed the key and turned it—an awful grinding sound howled from the engine. "Dammit!" he shouted, reprimanding himself by slapping the steering wheel lightly. "I always forget the engine is running!"

CHAPTER THREE

Kurt held Alice's hand in the backseat, squeezing it so hard at times she had to remind him by tapping his wrist. He'd release his grip a bit and give her a painful smile as apology, both of them too petrified to speak. When had he become incapable of protecting his wife? Where Alice was concerned, he'd always seen himself as an impenetrable fortress, a place she would always be safe, could always feel secure. But he hadn't protected her from the worst pain he'd ever seen her endure; their son's death. Now he sat in the backseat of a frightening stranger's sedan like a rebuked, powerless teenager.

He hadn't even put up a fight.

"What are we going to do, Kurt?" Alice whispered, seeming more composed. He squeezed her hand, trying to assure her they'd be fine, but he wasn't so sure.

"What do you want with us?" Kurt shouted toward the front seat, hoping the fear didn't bleed through his words.

"It would be almost impossible to explain," the stranger said. "But you're in no danger...not from me, anyway. I can assure you that."

"You entered our house uninvited, then tried to break into our bedroom, damn you!" Alice screamed, bolstered and trembling in the same moment, under a heady rush of adrenaline. Kurt tightened his grip on her hand, clamping her fingers with his fist. Alice glared at him, her eyes flashing darkly between resolve and terror.

The stranger sat quietly, steering the large vehicle, the two-lane road beyond the windshield a lonely, drab path carved into the darkness. It was several minutes before the stranger spoke again.

"I did that for your own protection," the odd man stated without emotion.

"Sure, that makes sense!" Kurt couldn't contain his sarcasm, scoffing from the backseat.

Alice kicked the back of the front seat, sending a brief and inconsequential wave through the upholstery that was quickly absorbed. It was enough to get the stranger's attention, their eyes meeting briefly in the rearview mirror, the man's and Alice's. The horror on Alice's face was torturous, feeding Kurt's rage, heating his blood.

"I wanted you to shoot me," the stranger said. "Once you saw you couldn't harm me, I knew you'd submit without any further skirmish. Until that little episode with the knife…. But I get it, you got to fight back a little, right?"

The interior fell silent, the road humming beneath Kurt's feet, his vision turning red focused on the man's silly fedora pocked with fresh holes. He hated this man; and hated himself in equal measure for not being stronger, braver. The image of the man's wrecked face played in Kurt's mind, the peculiar color of bone, almost metallic, the absence of blood.

"What in the world are you, mister?" Kurt blurted into the darkness. "You sure aren't human!" Leonard Nimoy's dark eyes peered out from the back of Kurt's mind, like a warning that Kurt should have watched more of those *Star Trek* episodes.

The man made a sound, as if about to explain, but fell silent. Leaning forward, the man pushed something on the dash that clicked. Less than thirty seconds later something popped and Kurt knew it was the cigarette lighter. The man slid a cigarette between his lips, then held the bright orange end of the lighter against the tip. Puffing a few times, the man cranked the window down with his left hand. Most of the smoke drifted away into the night.

After that, they rode a good long while without speaking, Alice propped against Kurt's shoulder, beginning to drift off to the gentle rocking of the automobile, as if her resistance had finally succumbed to the impossible situation. When the stranger turned on the radio, he was already on his fifth or sixth cigarette and Kurt elbowed Alice to wake her up.

"What?" she whispered.

"Buckle your seatbelt..." Kurt said, keeping his attention on the front seat, on the man's fedora, a slender ribbon of smoke trailing out the window.

"Why?"

"Just do it, dammit!" Kurt whispered, growing angrier by the second. The radio played music Kurt had never heard before. It was obnoxious, and hard to listen to. Alice found both ends of the belt and snapped them together.

"What about yours?" she whispered to him.

"Brace your feet against the back of the passenger seat," he said in a low voice only Alice could hear. "Down low."

When she moved her feet, he motioned for her to scoot them lower, where the seat was connected to the floorboards. When her feet were secure, Kurt took a deep breath.

"What are you going to do, Kurt?" Alice said, her voice shaky, rushed.

Kurt launched from the backseat, grabbing the man around the neck in a choke hold with his right arm, jerking him upward, backward, punching the man with his left fist. Alice screamed as the vehicle swerved right and left, tossing them back and forth in the seat. Every punch Kurt delivered felt like his knuckles landed against a brick wall. He didn't care. He tightened his right bicep into the man's throat, pulling him away from the steering wheel, punching him repeatedly until the huge sedan left the pavement, shooting from the shoulder, jouncing down the steep embankment. The vehicle crashed through saplings and shrubs, scraped over boulders, the terrain flashing with maniacal radiance under the bouncing headlights.

In the cacophony of twisting metal and shattering glass, the automobile came to an abrupt stop against a huge tree. Kurt was thrown forward into the front seat, holding to the man, smoke and dust filling the sedan. The radiator hissed, the sticky-sweet smell of antifreeze fouling the air. Kurt was confused, crumpled in the front seat, still holding to something in his arms. Alice sat limp, unmoving in the back seat, propped against the door, a jagged stripe of blood weaving down through her hair. Kurt glanced down at the object nestled in his crossed arms. When he loosened his grip, he saw that it was the stranger's head, wires and metal dangling from the severed neck, a few tubes dripping some kind of fluid. No blood. The man's body was smashed against the steering wheel, his chest crushed, his arms bent unnaturally. Kurt dropped the head to the floor and gave it a kick, trying to force it under the man's legs on the driver side. The head rolled back, the frozen eyes staring up at Kurt.

"Alice." Kurt reached over the front seat and undid her seatbelt, then pulled her flaccid body up trying to rouse her, shaking her. "Alice! Alice!"

She rocked her head with a dazed lethargy, her eyes partially open, unfocused. An orange glow flickered from the front of the car, hands of fire reaching out from under the crumpled hood. "Alice, come on, we have to get out!"

He pushed his door enough to jump free, then popped hers open, pulling her from the vehicle. She struggled at first, trying to get her bearings, like a newborn. He dragged her away from the billowing black smoke and bright flames. Alice stumbled behind him over the uneven forest floor, trying to keep her feet, the surrounding trees captured in a fierce orange light. When she fell, he jerked her upright and began pulling her down the steep embankment into the woods. She floundered, grappling with the difficult landscape, unable to maintain Kurt's pace. Just then the world exploded, throwing them forward, head over feet, tumbling down the hillside. Fire and ash filled the night sky, flames engulfing the automobile, illuminating the desolation around them.

Alice wasn't moving. Shaking and stunned, Kurt struggled to raise himself up on his right arm, his side burning, his left arm wet with something. The dampness was probably blood. He crawled over to Alice a few feet away and shook her, seized by a coughing fit from the smoke. Between hacking and choking, he tried to rouse her, feeling for a pulse, unsure if he was even holding her wrist correctly.

"Alice! Alice!"

He coughed again, then shook her when he was able to settle himself between spells.

"Alice, you have to get up!"

Alice moaned, her eyes fluttering, half-lidded. Her gaze fell on Kurt first, then shifted to either side as if trying to assess their situation. "What is happening, Kurt?"

"Can you get up, Alice?"

When he tried to help, she grimaced and squealed, then fell back into the leaves and sticks. "Something's not right, Kurt!"

"What hurts?"

"My back…"

She rolled onto her side, crying; a jagged stob, a half-inch in diameter, protruded from the blood-soaked spot on her blouse, just below her ribs.

"I'll be right back, Alice. Don't move!" He started back up the hill, hoping maybe he could get past the flames and check the man's glove compartment, or the trunk. Maybe find a first-aid kit. What was the point? The car was nothing but fire and smoke and charred metal.

He scrambled back down the incline, his shoes slipping on the loose dirt and dead leaves. When the intruder told them they had to leave, he'd at least given them a chance to get dressed. Kurt, maybe out of habit, chose his dress shoes; a terrible choice on this precarious scarp. Alice, at least, had slipped on her sneakers, the ones she always wore to work in the garden.

Alice had her eyes closed when he got back to her side. She seemed to not even notice his return. "Alice?" He spoke in an unhurried tone, not wanting to frighten her.

"Kurt?" She sounded weak, tired.

"I'm going for help…"

"You're leaving me here? How will you find me again?"

"The fire." He glanced over at the vehicle, the flames beginning to wane. Would he be able to find her again? He had no idea where they were. And if the fire went out, she'd be alone all night. "Do you think you can walk?"

She whimpered, reaching to her side. When she felt the stick, she yelped. "Oh, Kurt! Get it out!"

"I don't know what will happen if I remove it…"

"Pull it out, Kurt!"

Kurt shook his head, feeling as if she could bleed to death. He took off his shirt, then ripped away one of the sleeves, which he hoped would stretch around her torso to stanch the bleeding. She needed a doctor.

Alice continued mewling, eyes closed, her face pulled in pain. Kurt could hardly stand it. He reached down to the stick, gently pulling her blouse away from her skin, then raising it slowly over the top of the stob. Alice yelped again, convulsing in tears. "Is it out?" she screamed.

"One more second, okay..." Kurt's hand trembled, picturing the maneuver in his mind, telling himself to pull it out quickly. He was about to tell her what was coming, then reconsidered and yanked the stick free.

She screamed, then fell silent. Blood bubbled over the jaggedly-ripped skin like a weak geyser. Kurt wadded the shirt material against the wound with one hand, undoing his belt with the other. After stripping it from the loops of his trousers, he wound it around Alice's torso. At this point, Alice was no longer squirming or sobbing.

She'd passed out.

Kurt thought maybe that was the best thing. He sat back, checking his makeshift bandage. Blood blossomed though the shirt sleeve at first, just beneath the belt, then seemed to stop. He pressed his palm to the wound and was getting his breathing under control when a car slowed to a stop on the road above, the headlights burning a bright hole into the darkness. Car doors opened and slammed. The engine rumbled softly. For a brief second Kurt felt buoyed. Then, just as quickly, his excitement turned to dread when he noticed the man wearing a fedora and smoking a cigarette.

"Anyone down there?" he called from the shoulder. He was silhouetted against the headlight beams which glowed with a ghostly brightness in the smoke. Another man walked up next to him, also wearing a fedora and smoking. They spoke to one another, but Kurt couldn't understand what they were saying.

"Hello?" the man called again. Not waiting for an answer, the man scrambled down the hill. The other man remained behind on the road. Just then a woman appeared, smoking and strolling through the car beams in a dress, placing herself next to the man who remained topside. They spoke briefly until the man who came down the hill tried to approach the smoldering car.

"I can't see anything," he yelled up at them. "Too much smoke and fire. Contact command and see who had this sector. The man on the road spoke into a device on his wrist. Kurt was reminded of the Dick Tracy comic strip in the newspaper, Tracy communicating through the odd gadget that resembled a wristwatch. Kurt found the cartoon to be dim, and didn't really go in for all the crime drama and grotesque villains. And the idea that someone could communicate to someone else through a gizmo on their arm was just, well, silly to him.

When the man on the road spoke, he raised his arm and talked into his wrist, the apparatus glowing a pale green, then yelled down the name, *Kensington.*

"Okay, yeah, I know who that is," the man shouted up. "He had the Franklins. Kurt and Alison. If that couple is still in the car, they're goners." The man walked to the other side, giving the flaming automobile wide berth, then shouted up toward the road. "The passenger side door is open..." He paused to look around. "They might have gotten out." He sent his eyes in all directions, scanning Kurt and Alice's position several times but never locking on it.

"They may be on foot!"

The man on the road spoke into the device again, then nodded to the woman next to him. "Come back up. Command said they'll handle it from their end." The man standing by the charred sedan shook his head, as if disappointed, then labored up the steep slope, holding to shrubs and branches until he reached the road. When he crested the verge, an interlude of muffled discussion ensued, unintelligible to Kurt. A few moments later, car doors slammed, and the automobile eased away, picking up speed until it was gone. Kurt glanced over at Alice, relieved she hadn't witnessed the unsettling scene. How could those strangers know he and Alice had been in that car, and that their last name was Franklin? And what was Command?

CHAPTER FOUR

After sleeping for what felt like an hour, Kurt opened his eyes. Alice stirred. The woods were dark and gloomy, a pale fog drifting along the ground. Alice started shivering. Kurt scooted closer, trying to pat warmth into her arms. She curled into his chest and said nothing.

He rubbed his eyes, scanning the woods from one side to the other. The car had evidently stopped burning; Kurt could no longer see it in the fog.

"Do you think you can walk, Alice?" he said.

"I love you, Kurt." She smiled, her eyes sparkling in the darkness.

"I love you, too." He was nearly in tears over their mess, the strangers from the road loitering at the back of his regret. Should he have called out to them? What a fool.

"Can you help me up?" Alice said, pushing away from the ground.

Kurt jumped up, feeling better from the short nap, even though the cold was leaching away his heat. Walking would be good for both of them. He offered his hand to Alice. She took it with both of hers and grunted as he helped her to her feet.

"Which way, you think?" she said, grimacing at times, as if the pain came in bursts.

"Let's head down. Maybe we'll find a creek. Then we can follow it—"

"And get a drink! That would be good."

He nodded, then spun toward her, gripping her upper arms in his palms. "I'm so sorry, Alice. I should have—"

"No..." she said, cutting him off. "You saved our lives...now...let's just get moving..."

They walked without speaking, each sealed in their own thoughts, dead leaves crunching under every step. Kurt pictured the passersby who stopped on the road, the one who scrabbled down to check the wreckage. Kurt merely skulked in the shadows, afraid to call out. He dared not mention them to Alice as she would surely confront him on why he hadn't enlisted their help. He wondered the same, replaying what had caused him such trepidation. Something about them was off. Too well-dressed, maybe, all of them smoking. Both men wore fedoras, like the intruder who had kidnapped them. They looked nothing like any of his neighbors or friends, or anyone in Rescue for that matter.

Kurt led the way down the mountainside. Alice followed, branches occasionally snapping along the ground behind him. Alice stopped several times to lean her palm against a tree. Kurt sensed when she needed to rest, and paused, looking back to make sure she was okay. The sleeve belted to her waist appeared more bloodied than when they'd left the wreckage. Kurt retreated a few steps to check on her, fatigue dragging him down. Alice had her eyes closed, her head hung, her breathing strained.

"Let's sit," Kurt said, motioning toward a fallen log.

She shook her head, trying to slow her breath. "Keep moving, Kurt. Let's find water."

He nodded, though he knew she hadn't seen him, her

eyes aimed at the ground. "I'll check the bandage first," he said.

She shook her head, eyes shut, waving him forward. She coughed several times then pushed off the tree, looking past him down the dark slope. She pointed and waved again for him to keep moving.

They needed water, especially with her losing so much blood.

Kurt moved slowly, the descent treacherous, tedious, gravity waiting for any false step to send them down the escarpment. They had walked another twenty minutes or so when Kurt stopped. The woods were quiet, the fog not quite as thick. He spun toward Alice and motioned for her to stop. When she did, he heard the sound again, a low rumbling. Not mechanical, but steady. Maybe a waterfall.

"Can you hear that, Alice?"

She was seated on a large rock in front of a shallow cave, a natural stone overhang, her upper body bent into a ball over her legs. Kurt came over and sat next to her. "Alice, I think I hear water ahead. Can you go a bit farther?"

She looked up, trying to swallow, barely shaking her head. "I don't think I can, Kurt."

Her words wheeled inside his head, painting scenarios he was unwilling to face. He couldn't just leave her; he'd never make it back up this hill with water, even if he could find a way to carry it. And he couldn't just let them both die here in the dark. Maybe if they rested a while, she'd gather enough strength to get to the falls. Resting wouldn't stop the bleeding, though, but it could slow it. Why hadn't he called out to those people on the road? Would they be much worse off if the strangers had intended harm? He brought his eyes back to Alice. Could he carry her? She weighed no more than 110 pounds. In his youth he could have carried her across the entire county, but now....

He was unsure if he could lift her without upsetting her

wound? He went to the overhanging rock and started scrubbing his shoes across the earthen floor, clearing it for her to lie down, removing sticks and rocks. He walked over to her and rested his hand on her shoulder. "Alice, sweetheart, come over here and lie down."

She glanced at the spot he'd cleared, then raised her head to meet his eyes. "Just for a minute...or I'll never get up again." She struggled to her feet and forced a smile for Kurt. "How far you think?"

Kurt led her to the space beneath the carved-out rock. "Maybe a half mile. Maybe less..." He had no idea how far, or if they'd even get to it. If it was a waterfall he was hearing, then steep cliffs could certainly sit between them and the falls. They might even have to walk miles out of their way just to get down off the ledges, and risk never finding the water anyway. Alice didn't appear as though she had hundred feet left in her, much less several miles. The small cavern would provide protection for them if it rained. Maybe they should just sit tight until morning.

"Do you think you could hold onto my back?" he said, wondering if the wound was too tender.

She laughed, which prompted a coughing jag. When she got her lungs under control, she said, "A piggyback ride? You have to be kidding, Kurt. We'll both die out here."

"Let's try."

Her smile faded and she tried to stand, obviously struggling with how to initiate this move. Kurt came over and squatted down so she could climb onto his back. With her arms wound around his neck, he lifted her slowly, corralling her legs into the crooks of his arms.

She screamed in agony. "Put me down! Put me down!"

He squatted quickly, taking the pressure off her torso. She released his neck and stumbled back into the crevasse, flopping down on the ground, curling into a lump on her uninjured side. Her breathing came in huge swells, and Kurt felt helpless.

Minutes later, a bank of soundless lights slid past above the canopy of trees a hundred yards away. The lights rushed over the woods and disappeared from sight. Alice had her eyes shut and never saw them. Kurt eased in closer to her, placing himself beneath the huge rock outcropping. A few seconds later the craft returned. It paused, lingering high up, now only sixty yards or so from where Kurt and Alice rested. Completely silent. No way a helicopter could hover this close and they wouldn't hear it, Kurt thought. Then what was it?

When Reed was thirteen or fourteen, about four years before his death in 1962, he had called Kurt into the living room. Mike Wallace was talking on the television about flying saucers from other worlds, "…visiting our planet as we explore outer space with our rocket satellites."

"Is that true, Dad?" Reed said, chuckling, trying to make light of the report.

At the time Kurt hadn't known what to think, but he trusted Mike Wallace. Apparently, a former Marine Corps Major, Donald Keyhoe, had spotted several anomalous saucer-shaped aircraft flying in formation while he was on a mission. Kurt and Reed watched the report until Alice called them to dinner. Kurt never heard any more about it after that day.

Now, sitting beneath the rock shelf, he considered running out and trying to get their attention, whoever, or whatever, they were. What if the folks on the road had contacted the sheriff's office and this was a search party? A minute or so later, the lights edged away, a spotlight snapping on, burning down through the leaves and limbs. The craft crept off slowly, eerily silent. Once again Kurt entertained running out under it, waving his arms, but nothing felt right. He looked over at Alice, who was slumped against the ground. He felt horrible. Two opportunities to rally help and he'd passed on both, with Alice struggling for her life.

How could you be so selfish, Kurt Franklin?

He stretched out next to her on the ground, scooting up next to her back. With his arm lightly draped over hers, he held her close. She didn't move. He could feel her breathing as he slowly drifted off to sleep.

CHAPTER FIVE

The sky was beginning to color when he opened his eyes. It was early. Dew covered everything. Alice was still, but he could see her breathing. He eased back from her and strained to get to his knees. His ribs hurt when he tried to stand, the bump on his head starting to throb from being thrown into the kitchen table. He didn't think his ribs were broken, just badly bruised. He got up and grabbed a few leaves from a nearby shrub, bringing them over to her with great care. He squatted next to Alice's head, then removed some moisture from the leaf with his fingertip and smoothed it onto her parched lips. Her tongue slipped between her lips, welcoming the wetness. He held the other leaf to her mouth as she licked some of the dew. Her eyes opened and she smiled up at him. "I love you, Kurt."

He nodded, holding another leaf out to her. She took it and wet her face, then started to get up before he stopped her. "Let's check that dressing first," he said.

"No, Kurt. Let's get to the waterfall."

She was shaky as he helped her to her feet, but soon

righted herself, glancing at the gradually brightening sky. She motioned for Kurt to lead the way.

The thunder of water grew ever louder as they slogged down the mountain. They came to a clearing and eased down the embankment to a shimmering clear pool. They regarded one another, then took their attention to the thirty-foot cascade beating a froth on the water. Alice hurried to the water's edge and dropped to her knees, scooping water up to her lips, some of it spilling down her blouse, trickling down the sides of her mouth. She unbuttoned her blouse, carefully unwinding it from her torso before removing her jeans. The makeshift bandaged was nearly covered in dried blood as she entered the water, Kurt's belt holding it in place.

For a moment, Kurt could only gaze at her, how beautiful she was even after all these years. She looked like a child dragging water up her legs, to her belly, her underwear soaked. She bent over and splashed water on her face, letting it run down her arms.

"Join me, Kurt," she said, her face radiant.

The sun was tucked behind a distant hill as Kurt undressed and entered the pool in his boxers. It struck him as strange that neither of them recognized the surrounding mountains, the area void of signage, the landscape unfamiliar, foreign, desolate. Maybe they had traveled far north of Rescue, an area he was mostly unfamiliar with.

Streaks of sunlight spread into nearby trees and foliage surrounding the protected area. Kurt sloshed over to Alice. Some of the blood had faded from Alice's bandage, revealing the blue plaid pattern of what had been his shirt sleeve. He was studying the bandage when Alice took him in her arms.

"Thank you for not giving up on me," she said, giving him a light kiss.

"You're my life, girl," he said, hugging her loosely so

he didn't hurt her side. "But we need to change that dressing."

"Do you know we've never been on an adventure before?" she said, her head tilted back, eyes sparkling up at him.

They planned a few trips over the years, but it seemed every time they had the car packed, ready to drive to the mountains, or take a trip across country, something came up. Car trouble a few times, their boy Reed taking sick suddenly with measles, emergencies at the construction company Kurt worked at for a while as a heavy equipment operator. Only twice did they ever make it out of Rescue. The first time was to drive just over 900 miles to the Pacific Ocean when Reed was twelve. The second time was to go dancing at a bar and restaurant that had recently opened in nearby Destine. That was three years after Reed was killed in the tractor accident; both of them knowing they needed to move on with their lives.

"Anywhere is an adventure with you, Alice," he said. "I only ever wanted to spend every moment with you."

She rested her head against his chest and held him.

After several minutes, she took Kurt's hand and led him to the shoreline where their clothes lay in a heap. The sun had edged up over the distant mountain, bathing them in warm sunlight. Alice stood still as Kurt carefully unbuckled the belt, blood swamping the shirt sleeve, the wound a shocking reminder of the night before, rushing back with such ferocity Kurt felt faint.

"We need to stop the bleeding," he said, a bit woozy, tightening the belt back in place.

She smiled, glancing at the soaked sleeve, before bringing her eyes back to his. "I feel much stronger now. It'll be okay."

He nodded, life coming back to his own limbs, chasing the vertigo away. She wasn't normally prone to dizziness, or queasy stomach, never growing peaked or ill. He reached over and started undoing the belt again, being careful as he pulled the end out from under the keeper. He motioned for her to hold the bandage in place while he unwound the belt from her waist, then tossed it aside like a dead snake. He swallowed, afraid of what he would see when he pulled the soiled shirt sleeve away from the wound.

It wasn't nearly as ruddy as he'd prepared himself for. He guided her hand to the wound, and told her to press her palm against the gash, then lifted his shirt from the ground and whipped it in the air a few times to remove any sand and debris. He tore the remaining sleeve free from the shirt. He thought she should sit on the log while he replaced the bandage, so if she fainted, she wouldn't hurt herself falling.

"I'm not gonna faint, Kurt," she said, waiting. "I'm more concerned about you right now, the way the color's left your cheeks!"

"I'll be all right, girl. Don't you worry about me." He pressed the sleeve against the wound, then quickly tightened the belt.

"Whew!" she said, her eyes flashing as he cinched the leather belt to her torso. "Okay, so…now I may need to sit down." She chuckled as she lowered herself to a nearby log. After several deep breaths, she nodded, then frowned up at him.

"Are you in pain?" he said, finding a place on the downed tree next to her.

She shook her head. "Not really. Throbbing a little…but I just realized this is going to affect my expertise with the hula hoop!" She laughed.

For a moment Kurt had no idea what she was talking about. He scratched his neck, then smiled, picturing the colorful toy hoop hanging from the rafters in their garage. Reed, the first time he saw it on TV, just had to have one. They bought him one for his tenth birthday. But it was

Alice who first mastered the crazy thing, Reed saying, "Let me try now, Mom! C'mon, let me try!" The hoop would go once around his waist before ending up down at his feet.

"He finally got the hang of it," Kurt said, warmed by the memory. "Every day after school in the backyard.... Whew, that boy was not gonna be outdone by his mother."

"Janet helped him. Reed was so gangly then, but she was patient. Remember her, Kurt? She was a year ahead of him in school, and rode her bike over almost every day in the summer," Alice said. "It broke Reed's heart when she moved away a few years later." Alice sniffled.

When Kurt looked over, she was crying.

"I miss him so much, Kurt," she said, wiping her cheeks.

Kurt could only nod, himself at the edge of tears.

After a short rest, listening to squirrels chatter and squawk in the canopy of leaves above them, Kurt stood and asked if she was able to move on. She looked up at him, curious about the plan. He didn't have one, except for finding a phone to call Sheriff Logan, tell them of their strange predicament. Kurt wasn't even sure how far away their home was, or which direction to head to get back to it.

They started walking, following the creek down the mountainside. Eventually it should bring them to a road, or a farm or house. Something manmade. He tried to calculate how long they'd been in the car with Kensington before they ran off the road. A half-hour? An hour? It was impossible to tease out, the night a swirling mashup of irreconcilable events. For now, they had to pin their fate on following the creek and hoping to find a helpful stranger.

The woods grew more convoluted along the shoreline. At times, sheer rock walls forced them into the creek, water rising to their knees, one time to their thighs. Kurt glanced back often to check Alice's bandage, gauging the amount of new blood soaking the material.

When they arrived at the top of a plunging series of rushing cascades, they found it impossible to follow the water. Forced up the steep bank into the woods, they kept their eyes on the stream far below.

After they'd walked another hour or so, with no sign of the creek, Alice announced that she had to rest. They sat on a flat rock. Alice swiped sweat from her forehead and face. With eyes downcast, her mouth parted, her lips dry and cracked, she had the appearance of someone lost in the desert. He was about to tell her again how sorry he was, then met her eyes with silent regret. She returned a fleeting half-smile, then patted his thigh, her face flushed and drawn.

Alice had just closed her eyes when Kurt heard what he believed to be a dog. He glanced at Alice to see if she'd heard it too, though she showed no sign she had. When the bark came again, Alice's head rose up. "Could that be a hunter?" she said.

Kurt figured it could be, but was yet unable to get a bead on the direction. The barking continued, steadier now, until Kurt could clearly tell which direction it was coming from.

"Can you walk, Alice?"

She got up, nodding, her attention on the woods, the source of the barking. Following the disturbance—the sound of the yapping growing louder—they had only walked about fifteen minutes when they spotted a glade. By now the dog sounded frantic, at times howling as if in pain. When it caught sight of Kurt and Alice walking from the woods, the tenor of its cries changed, the animal running along the chain link fence, its tail wagging. Several times it jumped up, banging the metal fencing with its paws, its tongue hanging out.

Alice was the first to speak to the dog. Kurt took his attention to the back porch, expecting any moment for someone to open the door to check on the hubbub. Alice was petting the dog, asking its name, then checking its tags.

"Oh, Bella, aren't you just precious," Alice said, shuffling her hands along the dog's ears and shaggy neck. The dog licked Alice's hands, then her lips and cheeks.

Kurt regarded the exchange between Alice and the dog, wondering why no one from the house had come to check on these intruders at the back fence fussing with their Irish setter. Kurt walked to the driveway, then around to the covered porch in front. Bright red and yellow flowers in earthen pots lined the railing and stood sentry on either side of the front entrance. A late model, but well-maintained, two-tone Oldsmobile sat in the driveway. It was the kind of car Reed would have been proud to drive, and take a girlfriend to the diner, or roller-skating over in Destine.

Climbing the front steps, Kurt noticed the porch swing. Alice had always talked about having one, but they didn't really have the room; the swing would have constantly banged into the front windows, unless they used tippy-toes to barely move the device to and fro.

Before knocking, Kurt was suddenly aware of how he must look. Like a hobo trying to hitch a ride on the rail, or one being chased between coal cars by a gandy dancer. The plaid shirt had no sleeves, and his trousers were torn and filthy, falling down without his belt. He looked down at his dress shoes caked with mud and grime. He brushed his palms down his shirt, then hitched up his trousers and banged his bare knuckles on the hardwood door, sneaking a peek through the glass past the lacy white window shade. He waited, then knocked again, squinting through the lace. He reached his hand down to grab the door handle, activating the latch with his thumb, shocked when the door opened.

He quickly pulled it closed and rapped again, this time on the glass. Just then Alice came around the corner of the porch. "The car's in the driveway…" Alice stated, as if that were proof of the residents being at home.

Kurt nodded, studying the vague interior, sunlight from a set of slider doors at the back of the house illuminating the hallway. Alice joined Kurt on the porch.

"Did you try the doorbell?"

Kurt glanced at her, shaking his head, then sent his eyes back into the house. They both heard the bell when Alice pressed the button. They waited. Bella was barking again, probably set off by the bell.

"I don't think anyone's here," Kurt said.

Alice drew in a slow deep breath, holding her side, her expression darkening. She turned her head toward the road, surveying the rolling hills stretching toward distant trees. Kurt had done the same, and while the area was quite beautiful, it was, at the same time, terribly secluded. And unfamiliar.

Alice sighed. "Okay," she said. "There has to be another house close by…"

"What if someone's hurt inside?" he said. "Shouldn't we check?"

Alice's brow squeezed to sharp lines, her eyes slits. "What are you suggesting," she said, her mouth twisted with confusion. "Like…break the window?"

Kurt reached out and grabbed the handle, pressing his thumb to the latch. The door opened with a faint click. He held the door, giving Alice a questioning glance. From her pained expression Kurt could tell she wasn't wild about this idea. "We'll just go in and look around," he said. "That's all."

She sighed again, nodding him forward.

Just inside the foyer, the smell of fresh brewed coffee floated down the hallway. Kurt eased the door shut behind them, then called out. "Anyone home?"

Alice remained quiet, her eyes darting back and forth in the hazy light.

"Hello! Is anyone here?" Alice yelled. Bella's incessant barking in the backyard, though muffled, was further attenuated by the hollowness of the tomblike silence inside the house.

Kurt led the way down the hall, casually checking the dining room, the stately table covered in a pure-white lace tablecloth, six chairs with carved wooden backs, a bowl of fruit in a tole-painted tin bowl in the center. Kurt couldn't tell if the fruit was wood or real, but felt hungry enough to eat either. They went to the kitchen, spotted the coffee maker, steam rising from the pot of freshly-brewed. Kurt glanced back at Alice, her face pale, her eyes weak.

Kurt pulled out a kitchen chair and motioned for her to sit. He lifted the lid on the tin breadbox, finding a half loaf of Wonder Bread.

"No Kurt," Alice said, leaning on her arms at the kitchen table, her eyes half-closed.

"You need to eat something," he said, popping two slices into the toaster. He checked the cabinets above the sink for a plate, then brought down two coffee cups, filling them both, taking one to Alice. She closed her eyes and sipped the coffee black. Kurt returned with creamer and poured it into Alice's cup until the coffee was caramel-colored, just the way she liked it. When she was eight months pregnant with Reed (though they didn't know it was going to be a boy at the time), she had been sitting at the breakfast table and called him over. She had slowly poured milk into her coffee, both of them watching it change color. "That will be our baby, Kurt," she said, smiling up at him with tears in her eyes. He knew her meaning, even though his skin was hardly as dark as the coffee, and hers wasn't nearly as white as the milk. But Reed was just as she'd predicted; a beautiful young boy with the skin the color of caramel, and eyes radiant with blue light, just like Alice's.

Kurt was pulled from the wonderful memory when

Alice started protesting the thievery of helping themselves to these strangers' food. Kurt stopped her with a wave of his hand. "You have to eat, Alice. We'll make it up to them, but for now…" When the toast popped, Kurt spread it with Parkay margarine from the fridge, then set the plate and a jar of Smucker's plum preserves on the table, along with a knife and spoon.

"Please, just eat," he said. "Then we're going to take care of that wound."

Kurt could see Alice was starting to grow weary again and needed a boost. He went to the back door off the kitchen and opened it to let Bella in. The dog's paws slipped and slid on the linoleum floor as it rushed to Alice, barely pausing to acknowledge Kurt. Leaving Alice, the dog hurried to its dish, lapped at the water a few times, slopping it onto the floor, then hurried back to Alice.

Checking the cupboard, Kurt found several cans of dog food. He opened one with the electric opener and dumped the smelly glop into the dog's bowl across the kitchen. Bella gobbled it down within seconds, then lapped at the water bowl a few more times before returning to Alice. Kurt took the dog's bowl, rinsed it in the sink, then filled it with fresh water and sat it down.

Alice had finished her toast, color returning to her cheeks. Bella was sitting next to her, enjoying the ear rub, her tongue hanging out.

"You look tired, Alice," Kurt said, coming over to sit by her.

"I'm okay." Then after a short interlude, her hand massaging the dog's ears, she added. "Now what?"

"We need to get you to a hospital," he said. Their eyes caught, Alice's hand moving down Bella's neck, then back to her ears.

Kurt stood, and took a moment to steady himself. "I'm going to find the phone."

"There's one over on the far wall," Alice said, pointing with her free hand. "Past those pots and pans."

Kurt had seen the pots hanging from a metal contraption that looked like a chandelier, but had missed the phone. He went over only to find the cord cut, the way Kensington had cut theirs. Without explaining, Kurt left the kitchen to find another phone. He hurried up the stairs to the bedrooms, hoping to find one on the nightstand. Kurt recalled that Alice had always wanted a second phone in their bedroom; if they'd had one, maybe they could have called Sheriff Logan before that mad man Kensington broke into their house. He checked all the bedrooms, then headed back to the main level. Maybe they had a study. They did, full of shelves loaded with books, but no phone on the ornate polished desk.

When Kurt returned to the kitchen, Alice was asleep at the kitchen table, the dog lying next to her on the floor, its eyes darting between Kurt and some undefined vista in the room. He hated waking Alice but they needed to attend to her wound. Even if he found the owner's keys to the Olds, he wouldn't know which way to go to get to the hospital over in Downfall.

He scratched the back of his neck and poured himself another cup of coffee. Standing at the kitchen window, he let his eyes drift over the distant hills, fatigue filling him like warm liquid. In the backyard was a rusty swing set and some gardening tools. He went to the fridge to see what he could find for them to eat. Taped to the shiny surface of the freezer door were pictures of children, one with the parents standing next to them. A handsome couple, Kurt thought. The mother in the photo looked somewhat familiar, which felt odd.

Popping open the freezer door, he came across a few frozen entrees; Salisbury steak, mashed potatoes and corn TV dinner, some chicken pot pies, an opened box of Jeno's pizza rolls, which Alice had only bought once. He shut the fridge door and went back to the table to wake Alice. Bella didn't stir, just raised her eyes to Kurt.

He touched Alice's shoulder, whispering, "Hey, sweetie, you need to get up."

Alice woke with a rough grimace, then rubbed her eyes. "Kurt?" Bella got up on all fours and stretched, her eyes shifting between Kurt and Alice. Alice sucked at her teeth, running her tongue along the inside of her mouth. She looked peaked. Kurt placed his palm to her forehead. She was burning up.

Once he got her to her feet, he led her up the stairs to the main bathroom. Bella followed. Kurt closed the toilet seat and eased Alice down onto it. She was having difficulty keeping her eyes open. Kurt rummaged the medicine cabinet, finding aspirin, a needle and dental floss, peroxide and some ointment for cuts and abrasions. When he closed the cabinet door, he was dealt a shock by the grizzled old man staring back. He looked away, arranging the items from the medicine cabinet onto the bathroom counter. He filled a glass with water and helped Alice drink, then gave her two aspirin to swallow.

While explaining to her what he was going to do, he helped her off with her blouse and draped it over the edge of the tub. He found a clean washcloth below the sink, ran the water until it was warm, then soaked the cloth, ringing it out so it didn't drip.

"We have to clean it up, Alice," Kurt said, coming closer. "It's probably going to hurt."

She sipped the water again, then placed the glass on the window sill near the toilet. She smiled at him, then let her hand drift to Bella's shiny coat.

Kurt laid a towel over Alice's lap and told her to relax. She closed her eyes, her fingers combing through the dog's thick hair, the dog watching Kurt's every move with sad, pleading eyes, or so it felt to Kurt. He carefully loosened the belt and drew the soaked bloody sleeve away, dropping it in the trashcan. The gash wept instantly, dark blood pouring over the edges. Kurt dabbed the washcloth at first, trying to be gentle, cleaning the wound as best he could. He unscrewed the cap from the hydrogen peroxide and poured it on the wound. Alice tightened, but never cried out. The wound bubbled white and red. Kurt dabbed the wound with the washcloth, then more peroxide, the wound responding, fizzing, bleeding.

Before removing Alice's bandage, Kurt had sterilized the needle with matches he found in the bathroom drawer, then threaded the needle with dental floss from the cabinet. He had tried to bend the needle so it would be easier to stitch the wound, but to no avail. Alice seemed to be resting peacefully so far, but wasn't sure how she'd react when the needle went in.

The first prick was met with a slight jerk and a horrible grimace, but Alice didn't make a sound. Bella whimpered at first, nuzzling up against Alice's leg. Kurt worked with great care, wiping away blood as it gathered, using the peroxide liberally though knowing he wanted some left for when he finished.

Sweat prickled on Kurt's brow, Alice sitting patiently, her chest moving with each deep breath, occasionally sighing, or jerking when the needle pierced skin. Kurt was tying off the floss when Alice asked for her glass of water. "One second, doll," he said, knotting the tag end, then taking a deep breath as he reached up to the sill for the water. When she downed the last swallow, he refilled the glass. She drank the next one slower, but finished it all in four gulps. He was refilling the glass again when she sat up and inspected the stitches.

"That looks good, Kurt," she said, taking her eyes to Bella, gently squeezing her muzzle. "Oh, were you worried Kurt would mess up? He did a fine job." Bella wagged her tail.

Kurt applied antibacterial ointment, then made a nice

bandage from gauze and white medical tape. "Go lie down on one of the beds while I clean this up," Kurt said. "Here, let me help you."

"I'm okay, Kurt. Bella and I will find a nice place to rest."

Kurt rinsed the bloody washcloth, watching Alice shuffle from the bathroom, the dog at her side. The repair had gone well, but he couldn't be sure if they could keep the infection at bay. She needed professional care, someone to properly treat the wound.

He found Alice and the dog lying on one of the beds in a guest bedroom, smaller than the main one, but very nice. The owners were well-off. The idiocy of his statement hit him instantly; how could they be well-off? They'd been abducted! He was sure of it, the cut phone cord, the automatic coffee maker brewing the coffee on a timer, the car sitting in the driveway, the dog unattended, the front door unlocked. And possibly the couple wasn't faring as well as he and Alice. They could even be dead. The realization left him cold.

They needed to get going, find help before Kensington's bunch found them again. He hated to disturb Alice, but they needed to leave. Before he woke her, he decided to find the keys to the Olds. He searched the dresser drawers in the main bedroom, then the nightstands, the master bath. He went back to the kitchen and searched everywhere, then the foyer. Could the keys be in the car? He hurried out and checked the ignition, the visor above the steering wheel, the glove box.

Returning to the house, he remembered one night coming back from the Two-Step Tavern in Destine with Alice. Feeling a bit randy from the beer and dancing and music when they'd gotten back to the house, they hadn't wasted much time pulling their clothes off and jumping in the sack. The next morning, they searched all over the house for the keys to the Rambler. Alice finally checked Kurt's jacket pocket.

Rummaging through the owner's closet, Kurt finally found what he was looking for. He went back to the driveway and started the car, feeling a great relief that they didn't have to seek help bumbling though the woods. After shutting off the engine, he rushed back into the house, planning to wake Alice. She and the dog were already up, the dog growling playfully at her with its chew toy.

"We should have gotten a dog for Reed," Alice said, without looking away from Bella.

"There's a lot of things we should have done..." Kurt said, grimacing.

Alice stood and went over to Kurt. "You can't keep doing this, Kurt. His death wasn't your fault...or mine. It just happened. He'd driven the tractor hundreds of times..."

Kurt held her, his eyes on Bella at Alice's side, picturing Reed that day.

"I have the keys to the Olds," Kurt finally said. "We should hit the road."

"What about Bella?" she said.

"When her owners come home, they'll panic if the dog isn't here."

Alice gave him a sly, incredulous look. "Is that so? Won't they panic when they see their car is gone?"

"Yes, and maybe they'll call the police and we'll get some help!"

Alice nodded, amused, both of them knowing that wasn't going to happen; the owners weren't coming back.

"Maybe we should eat something quick," she said, getting up from the floor. "Anything in the freezer?" She made her way across the kitchen and stopped cold, studying something on the refrigerator. The photo of the couple and their two kids.

"What's wrong?" Kurt asked, easing over toward her.

She removed the photo from the freezer door, unable to take her eyes from it. "These are my parents…" she finally said, staring at the picture.

"What?"

"Look, these are my parents…but with someone else's kids…"

Kurt came over and studied the photograph, knowing they had looked familiar. "Are you sure?"

She spun toward him, eyes afire. "I know my own parents, Kurt! These are my parents…"

Kurt didn't have the energy to argue. Maybe they were, or maybe it was just a coincidence, or maybe they just looked like them. It was impossible that they could actually be her parents. Even so, he could sense Alice's resolve, which made him uncomfortable; Alice didn't suffer fools, or foolishness. Kurt didn't like what was going on. They needed to get as far from this house, from Rescue, or wherever they were, as soon as possible.

Chapter Six

When they reached the main road, Kurt swung the big Oldsmobile toward the distant mountains. He had no idea where they were going. Alice sat across the seat from him, her eyes closed. Though she said nothing, he wondered if she was in pain. Bella had coiled herself on the back seat, her eyes finding Kurt in the rearview mirror when he checked on her. She seemed quite content to be with them. Alice had taken food from the house for her, that they'd stowed in the trunk.

Twenty minutes into the drive, Kurt reached over and switched the radio on, content to listen to the station the owner had selected. Big band music from the thirties poured from the speakers. Kurt twisted the volume down, feeling a strange ambivalence about stealing the car. Alice hadn't pushed back much once it was decided the dog would come along.

His stomach rumbled and now he wished they'd cooked up a couple of TV dinners. Alice was all set to preheat the oven when Kurt felt anxious about staying in the house any longer than necessary. "Are you worried about the owners coming back?" Alice had asked while looking over the selection in the freezer. He said yes, though it made no sense; if the homeowners returned then at least he and Alice would have contact with someone, and maybe figure out what was going on. What bothered him most was Kensington, and the others on the highway who had stopped. Alice knew nothing about Kensington's head coming off in Kurt's arms. He still couldn't bleach that image from his mind.

"If we come to a roadside diner or something, let's stop and get something to eat," Alice said, looking over at Kurt. The sound of her voice brought Bella to life. The dog sat up in the backseat as if in agreement on the food stop. "I also need to use the restroom," Alice added, petting Bella's head, her arm outstretched over the back of the front seat.

Kurt agreed, though didn't hold out much hope. They'd been driving for nearly an hour and had passed nothing, not even a vacant house or dilapidated old barn. The most peculiar thing; they hadn't even passed another car going the opposite direction; they seemed to be driving away from civilization.

Something beyond the windshield caught Alice's attention, pulling her toward the dashboard, her eyes pointed up at the sky. "Can you see that, Kurt?"

"What are you talking about?"

"Just wait…it's behind that cloud right now…"

After a long interval, Kurt stealing glances upward, Alice shouted and pointed. "There! What the heck is that?"

It took a few seconds for Kurt to find the anomaly in the vast open space. Slowly, he eased to the shoulder for a better look, gravel crunching beneath the tires. When Alice popped open her door, Bella squeezed between the seat and the opening, joining Alice on the shoulder.

Kurt pushed his door open and climbed out, a bit stiff from the drive, or maybe it was all the walking. At fifty-five, he thought he was far too young to suffer the debility of old age. He hobbled around the front of the car waiting for the blood to reach his leg muscles, then joined Alice and the dog. He and Alice held their eyes on the bright object, while Bella sniffed the weeds along the edge of the road.

"I'll be damned," he said. "What the heck is that?" To Kurt's eyes it looked like a mini sun, not so bright they couldn't stare at it, but bright enough to have no real form, and too high to be a plane, he figured. Plus, it didn't appear to be moving. Nor did its luminance diminish. Like a new star, both miraculous and disturbing at the same time.

"Could be a comet," Alice said. "I saw something on the news the other night…"

"About comets?"

"It was after you went to bed."

"You didn't mention anything…"

"I don't tell you everything, you old coot!" She gave him a love-punch in the side, then called after Bella, who had wandered thirty feet or so down the road. The dog raced back. "Good girl," Alice said, ruffling the dog's ears. She opened the door and Bella squeezed through the space and took her place on the backseat.

Alice shut the door and looked up the road and down. "This is some kind of deserted place," she said.

Kurt wasn't about to tell her he hadn't seen anything since they started driving.

"I really have to pee," she said, looking around. She reached through the open front door window and grabbed some Kleenex from the glovebox and started down the hill off the road.

Kurt leaned against the front fender waiting for Alice to return, his mind grappling with the man in the driveway. Kensington. His silly hat full of buckshot holes. His ravaged head made of metal and tubes. A robot? Robots were the brainchild of Rod Serling and that Asimov fella. Robots didn't exist. Kurt's eyes slid back up toward the brilliant light in the sky. A comet? From outer space? Or maybe a flying saucer? Is that what Major Keyhoe saw nearly a decade ago? It didn't look anything like a saucer, and didn't appear to be moving. Kurt had no compartment in his brain to store such aberrations. As a heavy equipment operator and farmer, he knew the earth, the dirt and rocks, the sun and rain, natural things that endured, gave meaning to life. Were life.

"Ready!" Alice announced, coming up the shoulder to pull the Old's front door open. She climbed into the front seat with caution, protecting her wound, then closed the door, pointing her eyes out the windshield.

Kurt started the engine. "You doing okay?" he asked.

"Never better, Dr. Franklin," she said, smiling over at him. "You did a good job."

"No pain?" He looked at her side, the bandage hidden by her blood-stained blouse.

"None," she said, "but I can't say the same for my stomach."

He eased from the shoulder, not sure they would find food, or anything else, for that matter, which filled him with a constricting dread he'd never experienced before.

Chapter Seven

With the sky painted over in gray clouds, the gas gauge reading less than an eighth of a tank, Kurt could hardly contain his discomfort over their situation. Not a gas station in sight. To deepen the foreboding, he realized he had no money to buy anything, much less gas or food. His wallet sat on the nightstand in their bedroom. Kensington had told him he wouldn't be needing that.

Alice purred in the seat next to him, sleeping against the door. Bella lay in the backseat, soundless, eyes closed, both the dog and Alice unaware of how bad things were about to get. The dog had food in the trunk, but he and Alice had nothing. He never considered eating dog food before, but that unpleasant notion could quickly become a necessity.

The gray day turned to dusk, the needle on the gas tank hovering near the empty line, the road holding no promise of anything. One way or another, they'd be on foot again; no food, no coats, no protection from mountain lions or bears or wolves. The bleaker the situation turned, the more Kurt blamed himself for his stupid choices, wrestling with Kensington, causing the crash, not reaching out to the strangers on the road, not signaling the silent ship that had flown over them, its spotlight burning the forest in bright light. Anything would be better than this slow descent into ruin.

Alice yawned and smacked her lips, stretching her arms until her hands hit the headliner. Her eyes flickered a few times, then shifted toward Kurt. "Whew, I was out," she said, checking the terrain rushing by. "Man, it's nearly dark. Nothing? No restaurants?"

"Or filling stations," he said, hoping Alice would pick up on their dilemma without him having to announce it. "I thought I would have passed a Texaco or Gulf by now."

She leaned toward him to check the gauge. "Oh, boy. How much farther can we go, do you think?"

He shook his head, so mortified he almost broke into tears, wanting to apologize for getting them into this mess. How stupid could one old man be? "Not sure," he said. "I'm taking it easy on the speed, but these big old cars with those four-barrel carburetors guzzle the gas…you know how they are…"

She reached across the seat and laid her palm on his forearm. "We'll be okay as long as we're together, Kurt."

Did she really believe that? She wasn't exuding anxiety or apprehension, exactly, though something in her tone betrayed her lavish pronouncement.

Less than thirty minutes later, the engine knocked. The automobile lurched as the carburetor choked on the last of the fumes. The night outside the car was as black and undesirable as crude oil. Kurt guided the vehicle onto the shoulder until it came to a halt, the motor silent. Bella sat up in the backseat, excited to be stopping, as if this were a good thing. And to her it might be, but to Kurt it was the worst of all outcomes.

Alice pushed open the door and invited Bella to come out and stretch her legs. The dog bolted from the car and quickly squatted along the gravel shoulder. Alice leaned into the car, looking at Kurt. "Come on out. The air is fresh and cool," Alice said.

Kurt nodded, numb with remorse, and swung his door open. He ambled over to the shoulder and stood with Alice. "This is all my fault, Alice, and I'm so sorry." He let out a deep sigh, as if he'd just unloaded a dark secret that had been dragging him down for ages.

"That's nonsense, Kurt. You got us away from that crazy man…who knows what he had on his mind…. You saved us, Kurt."

He wanted to tell her everything—the people on the road after the crash, Kensington's robotic head in his hands, the tubes dripping some kind of viscous liquid onto the front seat of the sedan, the silent aircraft that flew overhead, searching for them—and maybe he would while they walked down the dark road toward whatever awaited them. And judging by the lightless terrain beyond the Oldsmobile—the wall of solid black stretching out to infinity—nothing good waited for them out there. Kurt had never known such hopelessness, except for when Reed was taken from them at seventeen. That was different, Kurt told himself; he and Alice had each other then, and they got through the aftermath of their son's death together. Now, with all that Kurt had left unsaid, all the chances to be rescued he had foolishly squandered out of paranoia, he felt alone in his self-reproach. It was eating him up.

"Let's sit in the car, Alice," Kurt said, going back to the driver's side door.

Alice let Bella into the back seat. The dog sat up, swiveling its head between Alice then Kurt, her tongue hanging out. Alice sat down, smiling at the dog before closing her door.

Kurt fumbled in the dark with the knobs on the dashboard. He pulled the switch for the headlights and the gauges lit up.

"What are you doing?" Alice asked.

"This car has hazard lights. I'm looking for the switch." When he found it, the hazard lights flashed intermittently. He turned off the headlights and they sat in the dark, the lights flashing on and off along the pavement beyond the windshield.

After a long silence, Alice asked, "What are we doing?"

"Waiting…"

"For what?"

"A car, maybe. Someone to come along…"

Alice folded her hands in her lap. The thick hush inside the car was held intact by the sporadic clicking of the hazard lights.

"How long will those last?" Alice finally said after an interminable stretch of time.

Kurt could only shrug. He had no idea.

"How many cars have we passed today?" Alice asked, Kurt knowing this was her way of moving him off his idea of waiting. It was useless; no one was coming.

"I have to tell you something, Alice."

"This isn't your fault, Kurt…"

"Just hear me out…" Kurt explained about the people on the road after the crash, the silent aircraft that had searched for them in the woods, how he had hidden them from the potential rescue. Alice sat without speaking when Kurt finished. He couldn't begin to know what she was thinking, and wanted desperately to end the excruciating silence.

"You probably made the right call, Kurt," she finally said. "But none of that matters now, does it? We have to deal with the situation before us…"

"We have no food, Alice! We're sitting here in the middle of nowhere with a stolen car! That's out of gas! And you need to be in a hospital! That's the situation we find ourselves in!"

After a few moments, Alice started laughing, causing Bella to yelp, then bark.

"What is so funny, Alice?"

Bella mewled and yelped.

"Just, that…this is some adventure, Mr. Franklin! Stolen cars. Lost in the middle of nowhere…nothing but dog food to eat!"

Bella barked again.

"Yeah, well, maybe next time we want an adventure," Kurt said with dire solemnity, "we go to the movies in Destine!"

At that, they both started laughing, Bella in the back seat prancing and barking.

"Settle down, girl," Alice said to the dog, smiling, rubbing her ears. "Everything's gonna be just fine."

Kurt felt a surge of relief; no longer alone with his bad choices.

With Bella lying down again, Alice said maybe they should try to sleep a while, then hit the road. "Looks like the moon is coming up. It'll be bright enough to see the pavement in a while."

Kurt nodded his agreement.

"And if that silent spaceship comes along, maybe we hitch a ride…!" Alice said, chuckling.

"I never said it was a *spaceship!*" Kurt protested, then eased off his indignation.

Alice opened the front door, pulled the seat forward and climbed in the back with Bella. "Come on, girl, let's get some sleep. We'll let Kurt keep an eye out for flying saucers!"

Kurt got out, went to the bathroom, then came back and stretched out on the front seat, his knees bent toward the dashboard, making a pillow with his arms. He was too big and too old for this kind of adventure, and he figured it would be impossible to sleep this way. He could at least rest his eyes.

CHAPTER EIGHT

When Kurt's eyelids parted, he was nearly blinded by the dazzling light burning through the windshield. His back was locked, pain shooting from his ribs when he tried to sit up in the front seat. It took a few seconds to remember where he was. When he did, he panicked, screaming for Alice to wake up. "They found us, Alice! Get up, we have to get out of here!"

"What? What's going on?" Alice said, her voice strained, confused, obviously still caught between a dream and waking.

Kurt forced himself up, everything hurting, and tried to leverage himself using the back of the seat, his long legs tangled beneath the steering wheel.

"We have to go, Alice! Get up!"

Bella started barking, jumping to the floor, then up on the rear side window.

"What the heck is going on?" Alice said, now fully awake under all the commotion.

"They found us!" Kurt screamed again, hurrying to find his shoes on the floor beneath the dashboard.

Alice leaned over the front seat and grabbed Kurt's shirt. "What are you talking about? Who found us?" she said.

"The airship I told you about!" Kurt shouted, pointing up toward the source of the light.

She looked up, staring out the windshield, then said, "That's the moon, Kurt. There's no one out there…. It's just the moon."

Kurt banged his head on the shifter coming up from his search of the floor. When he took his eyes out the windshield, he spotted the moon; a bright shiny quarter hanging in the night sky. It took several minutes to bring his heart and lungs back into line. Bella settled down, staying close to Alice.

"Come on, Bella," Alice said, "let's get you something to eat." The dog followed Alice out of the car. "Open the trunk, Kurt!"

It took a moment for him to find and release the latch. The trunk lid popped up with a jolt. Alice wrestled with things in the trunk while Kurt put on his shoes and tied them. He was so hungry that the smell of the dog food nearly made him sick to his stomach. He quickly rolled the window down and gulped in the fresh air, his neck stiff and painful.

She came around to the driver's side window and leaned in. "You can probably turn off the hazard lights," she said. "I don't think anyone's coming."

Kurt reached over and switched them off, putting an end to the monstrous clicking.

"We should get going, don't you think?" Kurt said, stretching his neck to the sides, then up and down.

Alice touched his neck. "Is it really sore?"

"It'll be all right."

"Should we take some of the dog food with us? Just the bag, not the cans."

"Sure. I suppose," Kurt said. "I can carry it." It was the

first time Kurt realized how thirsty he was. They needed to find water. And food.

Once they finished packing up, they started walking down the empty two-lane highway, Alice holding the flashlight from the glove compartment. Bella padded right at her side, Kurt following behind carrying the bag of dog food.

They walked for about an hour before they took a break by an old downed tree just off the road. The moon illuminated the surrounding terrain, making it easy to find their way. Kurt was still tired, though his neck was feeling better. He turned to Alice, wondering if the walk was bothering her wound. "How's the gash?"

"Fine. I feel it once in a while, but it's fine. I don't think it's infected."

Bella sniffed around the downed tree, then the rocks, never venturing far from Alice.

After a short rest, they resumed their trek along the shoulder of the road. Before long, Kurt spied the moon reflecting off a metallic object about fifty yards in front of them. He stopped, telling Alice to stop as well. He listened. "I think that's a bridge."

"Yeah, sounds like water," Alice said.

When they reached the structure, they wasted no time scrambling down the embankment to the edge of the stream. Alice cupped her hands and drank, Bella lapping nonstop at the water's edge. Kurt drank, then scooped water onto his sweaty neck, the water running down his back, wetting his shirt. Kurt felt a sense of peace, the urgency of hunger and thirst passing. No sooner had the calm filled him, when it was chased away by the sound of distant voices. Not only distant, but jarring, amplified, as if issuing from a loud speaker. Alice and Kurt stared at one another for just a moment before Kurt scrambled back up the slope to get a better look, telling Alice to stay put with the dog. He had just spied the lights in the sky when Alice appeared at his side, the dog prancing nervously next to her.

"Is that what you saw the other night," Alice asked.

Kurt nodded, the sound of the loud speaker drawing closer. "Can you tell what they're saying?"

"Not sure."

The hovering ship seemed to be a few miles off. They had been walking for over an hour. Kurt had once read in Readers Digest that the average walking speed of an adult was between 2 to 4 mph. Using that guide, he figured maybe they had gone a little over 2 miles, considering their age. Neither of them were fast walkers. So, it was conceivable that the craft could be near the abandoned Oldsmobile, searching it, possibly looking for them. When the ship appeared to start moving toward their current position, Kurt hurried Alice and the dog back under the bridge.

The craft was apparently following the highway, the huge spot of light crawling toward them along the pavement. In seconds it stopped just above the bridge, the light sprawling out to both sides, burning the exposed parts of the creek and shorelines in blinding light. The three of them huddled closer in the shadow of the bridge. Kurt felt around for a sizable stone, coming up with one the size of his fist. With his free arm, he pulled Alice closer, while Alice hugged Bella in both arms.

"Kurt and Alice Franklin, you are in grave danger," the disconcerting voice bellowed from above. *"We want to help you. Please show yourselves."*

Alice looked back at Kurt, who was shaking his head no. The voice, however, was causing Bella distress, the dog fidgeting in her arms.

The warning came again; *"Kurt and Alice Franklin, you are in grave danger. We want to help you. Please show yourselves."*

Bella fought Alice's grip, wriggling its way free of her

control. In seconds the dog was up the hill, barking at the craft hovering above the bridge.

"I'm sorry, Kurt," Alice said. "I couldn't hold her.'

Would the ship land on the bridge? Could it land, or would it go to the field on the other side of the stream? Bella's fevered barking had not subsided one bit. Maybe they should make their escape while Bella had them distracted?

"Alice, let's run for those trees," Kurt said in a low voice, pointing her attention up stream.

"What about Bella?" she said.

"We can't worry about her right now."

She nodded, clearly disappointed. He took her hand and helped her up, easing her toward the edge of the bridge abutment, still hidden in shadow. It appeared to be about fifty yards to the edge of the trees. "Don't look back for anything," Kurt told her. "You ready?"

She nodded, taking a deep breath.

"Kurt and Alice Franklin, you are in grave danger," the voice boomed again. *"We want to help you. Please show your-selves."* Bella barked more fervently and Kurt could almost imagine her jumping up at the craft, the way she banged against the fence when they approached her yard.

Kurt dashed out first, Alice following. The woods were coming closer. Another hundred feet...fifty feet...thirty feet...almost there, when Kurt went down. Alice hurried over to him. "Are you okay?"

"Keep going and don't stop. I'll catch up to you!"

She grabbed his hand, pulling at him to get him up. He was pushing off the ground with her help when he took his eyes to the bridge, the ship appearing enormous, hovering no more than fifty feet above it, the Irish Setter agitated but dwarfed by the huge vessel. When Alice caught sight of it, she stopped. "What in the world is that thing, Kurt!"

"Come on. Let's keep moving," he said, getting his feet under him. "We have to keep moving!"

Within seconds they fled under the massive canopy of trees, limbs and leaves. Kurt led the way up the gradual slope, following the stream, winding them through tangles of small trees and bushes, weeds and boulders, sticker bushes picking at their clothes, slowing their progress. Kurt spotted a narrowing in the creek, a place they could cross without too much effort. Kurt entered first, the water to his calves, then his knees. Alice followed, both of them high-kicking, battling the current. When they reached the other side, Kurt led them away from the creek, trying to parallel the highway, though now at least a quarter of a mile from it. Alice caught up to him and grabbed the back of his shirt.

"I have to stop," she said, her breathing ragged, coming in desperate gulps.

Kurt led them to a huge boulder where they could rest. Until they sat, he hadn't been aware of the pounding in his chest. They had only been stopped a few seconds when the light from above broke through the thick cover of leaves about fifty yards from them. It passed soundlessly, seemingly following the stream up the hillside. The warning issued again, this time muffled by distance and the understory, though clear enough to still understand.

"Kurt and Alice Franklin, you are in grave danger," the muted voice claimed. *"We want to help you. Please show yourselves."*

They watched as the spotlight fragmented through the branches and limbs, appearing like frenetic lightning, until it vanished, the voice echoing back subdued and foreign, overwhelmed by the vast wilderness. By now they had both caught their breath, ready to start moving again.

"Grave danger?" Alice said. "What's that about?"

Kurt cleared his throat, his attention on the retreating

lights. "I have no idea, as if this night couldn't get any stranger."

"I'm worried about Bella," Alice said.

"She'll be all right. She's a dog. Her instincts will take over."

Kurt led the way, pushing aside branches, trying to clear a path for Alice, warning her anytime he was about to release a recalcitrant limb so it didn't lash across her face. He hated leaving the stream and the clean water source, but their only hope was to get back to the highway, which would eventually take them into a town. *Eventually.* That was the tricky word...*eventually;* they could exhaust their stamina before *"eventually"* ever kept its promise of salvation.

They'd walked for nearly two hours with no traffic, making it impossible to know if the highway was near or far. Kurt stopped when they came to a spring, so they could get a drink, wipe the sweat from their faces, clean the dirt off their arms. Alice knelt on a patch of ferns, drawing water up to her mouth, then her face, wiping the crud off her arms.

"It's getting light out," Kurt said. "Let's rest here a while. Maybe we'll be able to see better."

"What are we looking for?"

"The highway."

"The highway? They'll be able to find us on the highway...whoever *they* are..." She chuckled, as if the thought of running from an unknown threat was somehow funny.

"There's something I didn't tell you, Alice," he said. "But you need to know." He started telling her about Kensington, how he'd grabbed the stranger by the head, forcing them off the road and down the culvert.

"I know," she said. "So?"

"What I didn't tell you was that his head...his head came off in my hands..."

Even in the dingy light, Kurt could see Alice was confused by this new information. "I don't understand."

"He wasn't human, Alice. He was like made of metal or something, tubes and metal parts dangling from his neck…"

"You must be mistaken, Kurt. We were shaken up…the light was bad. You must have been tricked by the circumstances. It was very traumatic, crashing like that. Then the fire—"

"I know what I saw, Alice. That man wasn't human."

"What are you saying…like a…a robot or something?"

"I don't know, but he had no blood running through his veins. There wasn't a drop of blood anywhere in that front seat. That's all I'm saying."

Alice was quiet, chewing on this new information, her face a puzzle of sharp angles.

"That's why we're running from these…things, whatever they are."

Kurt found a patch of leaves and stretched out on the ground. After a few minutes, Alice got up and joined him, snuggling in close to him, welcoming the heat, and reassurance. Soon, both were asleep.

Alice woke first, the sun cutting through the leafed-out trees above them. "Hey, Kurt," she said, shaking him. When he didn't stir, she got to her feet and walked into the thick cover, then pulled her jeans down and squatted to pee. When she finished, she turned to see Kurt pushing up to a sitting position, his eyes searching for her.

"I'm here," she said, coming out of the thick brush.

"You, okay?"

"I'm fine. You?"

"Stiff as a stick! When did I get so out-of-shape?"

She smiled, then helped him up. "This adventure is a bit beyond our scope of activity. I'm feeling it too. I can't remember the last time I actually *ran!*"

"Well, maybe so, but you look spry as a teenager," Kurt said.

They each scooped a few drinks from the spring, then headed out, Kurt's eyes fixed on the position of the sun. He was no seasoned outdoorsmen, but he knew the sun rose in the east, and the highway ran north and south, at least the stretch they'd been on. If they headed toward the sun, they would almost surely have to cross the highway at some point. Unfortunately, nothing was that predictable in the wilderness. But they had no choice but to try his plan. Otherwise, they could end up meandering in circles for days, making no progress whatsoever.

Kurt was just about to call for another brief rest, when something came charging through the underbrush. Alice heard it to. She picked up a large rock and stood by Kurt, who had found a hefty limb and had it positioned over his shoulder like a club. Mountain lion was the first image that popped into his mind, or maybe an enormous raging bear. Seconds later, an animal broke through the weeds and saplings, headed directly for them. Kurt was just about to swing the limb when he saw it was Bella. Alice squealed with joy, squatting down to take the brunt of Bella's excitement.

"Oh, look at you," Alice gushed, shuffling her fingers along the dog's ears and scruffy neck, the dog jumping up on her, licking her face. "You had me worried!"

The dog broke from Alice and rushed over to Kurt to give him a sniff, then jump up on his legs. When the love and attention did not return, she dashed back to Alice. "Don't worry about him," Alice said to the dog. "He has a hard time showing love, you beautiful girl." Alice smiled up at Kurt, who was frowning. Maybe under different circumstances, he was certain Bella's advances would not have been met with indifference, but he couldn't muster any enthusiasm for the animal at present. Unfortunately, in their harried escape from the airship, he had left the bag of dog food under the bridge.

The sun had climbed high overhead by the time they first laid eyes on a treeless swath through the forest. It had to be the highway. They had yet to lay eyes on actual pavement, but what else could it be? Maybe railroad tracks, which was just fine. Maybe even better; it would surely take them to a station or town.

At the base of the incline, with the clearing above them, they struggled up the steep embankment to find a two-lane paved road. The shoulder of the highway provided a comfortable walking tread, mostly flat. The sun beat down, the air growing hot with humidity. Though he held out little hope for a passing car, he refused to rule out the possibility. What were the odds in this remote area, or anywhere else for that matter, to never once encounter a passing car on a highway this well maintained? It was certainly built to go somewhere, he reasoned.

Alice was in her glory with Bella at her side. She often talked about getting a dog, but Kurt had not wanted the added responsibility, though at times he thought it might be nice to have one lying by the fireplace.

A sign ahead gave Kurt a burst of energy and hope. Finally, an indication of civilization. But the euphoria gave in to suffocating exasperation when the signpost warned, ROAD OUT AHEAD. Road Out? Did that mean it had washed out? Like from a storm? Why had no one fixed it? If the road truly was out, that would certainly account for the lack of traffic. Kurt exhaled, frustrated, wondering what they'd find over the next little hill beyond the sign.

It was far worse than he'd imagined. A ten-foot chain-link fence crossing the road and dropping down off the shoulder into the woods on both sides, with concrete barriers, painted yellow, sitting in front of it, blocking the highway completely. Beyond the chain link, nothing but huge boulders and rocks, weeds and new saplings and a few older trees. No cracked or washed-out pavement, no cleared dirt where a road could've been. It appeared to Kurt that the road wasn't *out*, but more likely, had *never been!* He worked with earth moving equipment plenty in his life, and knew a road had never stretched beyond that barrier.

He stood shaking his head, unable to comprehend why anyone would just stop a road in the middle of nowhere.

"What's going on, Kurt?" Alice asked, walking up beside him.

"Beats me. I've never seen anything like it."

CHAPTER NINE

Bella sniffed the bases of the concrete barriers, then padded over to the sprouts of weeds along the bottom of the fence.

Kurt was stymied, disheartened, unsure what to do. Not to mention hungrier than he could ever remember. But he kept that to himself, knowing Alice had to be just as famished. He tried to ascertain how far the chain-link fencing dug into the woods on either side of the highway. He couldn't tell from where they were standing. Maybe some kind of compound. Yet there were no KEEP OUT signs bolted to the fencing, or warnings about trespassing.

"I need to see if we can get around this," Kurt said. "I'll be right back."

"We're going with you. We need to stick together."

She was right, but he hadn't wanted to subject her to unnecessary walking, asking about her wound before they climbed back down the steep embankment.

"It's fine, really," she said. "Stop worrying about me. I don't need protecting, Kurt."

Bella fell in next to Alice, with Kurt leading the way, paralleling the fencing into the woods. It ended abruptly about 150 feet in. Kurt crossed past it, wondering why in the heck the engineers had taken it this far from the road. No car could ever leave the pavement without getting stuck, and anyone on foot could easily get across to the other side.

"That was weird, huh?" Alice said as she and Bella caught up to Kurt.

"Has there been anything that wasn't?"

Alice chuckled, then walked up behind Kurt and wound her arm through his. He stopped and turned toward her as she pulled him close. "I don't think we've hugged in days," she said. She pushed up on tiptoes and kissed him on the lips. When she drew back, she said, "I love you, Kurt."

He nodded, thankful for his good fortune at having ever met her. "I love you so much."

They had just started walking when they came to a clearing. Alice pointed off to the east. "What's that?"

"What are you talking about?" he said.

She eased up closer and pointed toward a space in the trees. "That. See it? It looks like smoke."

He jogged his head back and forth until his eyes caught on what she was seeing. "I'll be damned! If that isn't a forest fire, I think we found some civilization."

Buoyed by the new discovery, Kurt walked more briskly, the hunger pangs taking a backseat, his worries over nightfall gone. In the cool shade of the forest, he was hopeful they could reach the smoke in under five hours if they didn't take too long of breaks. Alice was invigorated as well, having no trouble maintaining Kurt's new pace.

Dusk was approaching quicker than Kurt had anticipated. They had walked for several hours, and though the smoke was much closer now, it was still at least another hour or two away. Distances were deceiving in this part of the country, especially when the terrain opened up into seemingly infinite vistas with nothing to measure against. And with the low humidity—which did make the walking more pleasant—even the most distant mountain range could appear much closer than it actually was.

Kurt stopped and sat on a huge slab of stone. "Let's rest here."

Alice sat beside him, while Bella explored the new terrain, her nose tracing unseen paths along the ground.

"I don't think we're very far, now," Alice said, placing her palm on Kurt's thigh.

Kurt didn't dispute her assessment; what was the point of telling her they wouldn't reach it before nightfall. And that was only if they could guide themselves by the lights of that distant city which should stand out like a new planet in the dark. And maybe she was right, that they were closer than he figured. Even so, he was unable to stop wondering how cold it would get once the sun went down. It had already started cooling off. With their arms sunburned, they would be susceptible to chills and an uncomfortable evening, or worse, hypothermia.

He kept all of that to himself.

Alice was a trouper, staying up with him through the dark, never asking to stop or rest, never complaining about being hungry, or tired, or hurting. The slog had been grueling, deep culverts hidden between seemingly flat expanses of forest, the rocky tread wreaking havoc on their knees and ankles, coupled with the constant ache of hunger. It was her resolve to keep moving that helped to bolster his own spirits and push him onward.

Hours later, finally arriving at the dismal city—which wasn't a city at all, but more of a compound of some kind —they faced their last impediment to a hot meal and some much-needed answers; a twelve-foot-high chain-link fence with barbed-wire stretched along its upper edge. What were they trying to keep out...or in?

While Kurt and Alice discussed what to do next, Bella

appeared on the inside of the fence, sniffing the weeds along the lower edge.

"How did you get in, girl?" Alice said, smiling. "Show me!"

Bella jumped up on the fence, then sprinted along it, quickly squeezing under it about twenty feet away and was soon back at Alice's side. "Good girl! I wish I had a treat to give you!"

Bella led the way back to the egress beneath the fencing and appeared on the other side. Alice had to tunnel out more dirt in order to squeeze beneath it. Once she made it under, she started digging it deeper for Kurt. Bella, energized by this new enterprise, joined Alice in digging beneath the fence. Kurt helped from his side and the three of them were soon headed toward the brightest lights, trepidation turning Kurt's legs to jelly.

Nothing so far appeared inviting about this place and his dread deepened. It was nothing like what he expected, or hoped for. At the complex's center, rose a multi-level concrete block of a building, some five or six stories high, with smallish windows. More like a bunker than anything he'd ever seen. Positioned at numerous locations within the compound surrounding the building stood tall smoke stacks made of concrete or brick, piercing the gray sky, a few of them belching out white or gray. A factory of some sort, Kurt figured. But no people milling about. He'd never witnessed anything like it. The smell was awful, like spoiled milk and toxic chemicals. A desolate place to work and live.

"Do you smell that?" Alice said, her thumb and forefinger pinching her nose shut.

Kurt looked around, spotting an open gate, and more buildings beyond that. "Let's check out that gate."

Just as Kurt and Alice started toward the entrance, two men wearing blue coveralls walked to the gate and stood a moment, joined by two others dressed the same. Some kind of uniform, Kurt figured. A moment later, two huge trucks followed by three blue buses rumbled toward the gates, honking and flashing their lights for the men to move out of the way. The men ended up on the far side of the small convoy, out of Kurt's view. Once the vehicles cleared the gates—their departure marked by a swirling cloud of dust—Kurt and Alice heard shouting over the dying grumble of the exiting motorcade. As the dust settled, the crowd of men, all in blue coveralls, had entered into an unholy brawl, shouting and pushing and punching, with more men in blue rushing over to join the melee.

Kurt and Alice shrank back behind the small building near the fence, away from the flood lights illuminating the yard. They could see everything from the shadow side of the small metal building. A couple of men had huge knives, like machetes, that flashed under the lights as they slashed at the crowd. A siren sounded, bringing guards in dark uniforms with long black sticks. When they pressed the stick against one of the brawlers, the hooligan would fall instantly, as if dead. The guards disbursed the crowd quickly, many of the fighters lying unmoving in the dirt. A truck pulled up and more guards jumped out to load the unconscious, or deceased, into the truck. When they cleared the area, the truck sped away.

"Maybe this is a prison," Kurt whispered to Alice. Alice remained quiet, squatting down to hold Bella.

Two more blue buses—filled with passengers, mostly men, their pale, blank faces staring from the windows—raced by the metal building headed for the front gates. Then three more trucks and another blue bus, all of them speeding through the compound and disappearing down the road, the vehicles and their red taillights consumed by a towering cloud of dust.

"We need to go back under the fence and walk around the compound until we can find a more suitable environment," Kurt said, "if one exists."

They had just started to walk back toward the egress under the fence when a man in blue coveralls spotted them. "You wait! You stop!" the agitated man shouted, hobbling toward them. Kurt could tell something was off about the man, with his mind, not only by how he spoke, and his clumsy gait, but something Kurt intuited, but couldn't quite figure out.

The man was cutting off their path to the fence, when Bella bolted from Alice's grip and lunged at the man, knocking him over, and attacking him. The man screamed and yelped and tried to fight her off, but to no avail. Bella growled with the man's arm lodged between her jaws. Alice was about to call her back when another man came on the scene and started slashing at Bella with a machete. Snarling and barking, Bella abandoned the downed man and lunged for the machete man, only to die quickly, barely a yelp, when the man cut her head off. She fell to a lifeless heap on the ground. Alice expelled a muffled shriek, her hands pressed over her mouth. The machete man walked closer to Bella, kicked her body with his boot before wiping the blade of his huge weapon on the dog's fur. He glanced over at the man Bella had attacked, then walked away, leaving the bloody man writhing in pain.

Kurt could only shake his head, holding Alice close, who trembled in his arms. When he thought it was safe, Kurt led Alice back toward the egress in the fence, her once-soft features ruined by her tears. Kurt moved slower than he would have liked, keeping to the shadows, being extremely careful with Alice—her legs barely moved, as if made of wood.

CHAPTER TEN

After helping her to the small culvert they'd hollowed out beneath the fence, he implored her to get through it before anyone else came. She was despondent, and fell against the fencing, sending a tinny shiver of agitated metal through the solitude, which attracted the attention of the man with the machete. He raced from the shadows toward Alice. Kurt acted fast, tackling the man, screaming for her to get to the other side. Alice snapped from her torpor long enough to squeeze through the opening.

Kurt punched the man repeatedly with his free hand, holding the machete at bay with his other. Once Alice was on the other side of the fence, Kurt wrestled free of the man, then kicked him before diving for the shallow tunnel. He had just made it through when the man with the machete lunged for him, trying to grab Kurt's foot. Kurt jerked it away, scrambling to his feet. Unable to latch onto Kurt, the man started belly crawling beneath the fencing, Kurt unaware he was so close.

That's when the unimaginable happened.

Kurt looked for Alice. She was gone. The man with the

machete struggled on the ground, his coveralls caught on the sharp metal tines. Alice appeared, seemingly out of nowhere, like a flash, with a huge rock hoisted above her head. She brought it down on the trapped man's head once, then again, then several more times before Kurt could believe his eyes. By the time Kurt reached her, she was on her knees, the stone above her head, coming down again, the man's head nothing but a dark, ruddy pulp.

Kurt grabbed the stone away from her and helped her to her feet. She was shaking, her eyes bright and round in the black night. Her hands resembled claws at her sides, as if in her mind she was still holding the rock. He pulled at her to get her moving, her head turned back, her eyes unwilling to release the dead man.

When Kurt managed to get them far enough away from the compound, he stopped. Alice collapsed to the forest floor and curled into a tight ball, her hands, jeans and blouse stained with blood. Kurt looked around, listening carefully for anyone who might have followed them. He figured they'd be safe, at least for a while. Hopefully until daybreak.

After surveying the dusky woods one more time, he shifted his attention down to Alice. Her eyes were closed. Maybe she was asleep, or in shock. Regardless, she wasn't moving, and Kurt didn't know what to do. The woods surrounding the compound had turned too treacherous to navigate in the moonless night. He nestled down near her, conscious of the threat that someone could come along. Occasionally, when the breeze changed direction, the stench of the compound reached them.

Sometime later, while replaying the ghastly incident, Kurt glanced over at her lying in the dead leaves. The gravity of the event had been too much and she hadn't moved since they arrived at this small clearing. Maybe, like him, she was weak from hunger, and the shock of what had happened overwhelmed her. He needed to find food, and water, then figure out what to do. Once the authorities found the dead man, they would surely send out a search party to hunt the killer. Kurt realized he had left Alice's bloody rock lying where he'd wrenched it from her hands. Bill Logan, the sheriff of Rescue, explained to Kurt once how he'd assembled a search party to look for a teenage girl who'd gone missing. "Searched day and night," Logan had told him. "The dogs finally found her at the edge of a creek. Nothing nefarious. She'd been hiking and got bit by a rattler, the coroner said. Just bad luck, poor thing."

Lawmen with bloodhounds and hunting dogs? He and Alice wouldn't stand a chance of evading them. How could they explain why they'd been at the compound? The man with the machete had seemed set on killing them, but maybe he was a guard, and was trying to arrest them. They had, after all, been trespassing. He couldn't let Alice go to jail for saving their lives. Even so, he still had a hard time accepting that Alice had been capable of such an atrocity, even given the circumstances. And the authorities; how would they see it? Self-defense? Or murder? Kurt couldn't begin to untangle the mess they found themselves in.

His stomach grumbled, bringing him back to the most pressing order of business.

Food.

How much time would they have before the police came looking for them? Alice hadn't moved or made a sound. He didn't want to wake her, but felt he couldn't wait for her to get up. Was she in shock? He had no idea. The only thing he knew for sure was that they needed food and water. And the only place he figured to find some was the compound. If he could just leave her a note.

He pushed himself up to his feet, searching the surrounding area for something to write on. Finding nothing, he picked up a short stick, then cleared a patch of dirt, sweeping the debris and leaves to the sides with the edge of his shoe. He pressed the stick hard into the dirt, the space just large enough for two words. STAY PUT. In letters ten inches high. He hoped he could get back before she woke. That would be the best outcome. The second best; that she saw the note…and heeded it.

The next challenge was finding his way back to her once he secured food. Maybe if he broke branches as he made his way back to the compound. He would also try to scuff up his path, make it evident. He strode over and kissed Alice on the side of the face, near her ear, stealing a whiff of her hair. He loved her smell. "Please don't leave here, baby. I could never go on without you."

She didn't stir, silent as the ground she was curled up on.

Kurt set off, a sickly dread pooling in his gut. He snapped limbs at eye level as he eased forward, checking back often to see if Alice had awakened. In less than a minute he had completely lost sight of their small clearing, and was already doubting where he'd left her. How would he ever find their spot again?

The sudden disorientation made his stomach lurch.

He started back toward her, checking the limbs he'd broken, or bent. In seconds, he spotted her, motionless as a log. He hadn't gone more than *twenty feet* from the spot! He would never find her again if he went all the way to the compound. Panic shot through him, weakening his resolve. They couldn't keep running without food. But he couldn't chance getting separated from her.

He reached into his pants pocket, bringing out the roll of first aid gauze he'd stolen from the house so he could change Alice's dressing. He ripped the first three feet into small pieces no more than six inches long, tucking the rest of the roll into his pocket.

Even in the dark, the white strips marked a clear path as he moved through the woods. From time to time he'd pull the roll out, rip a length of it into small strips, then affix them to branches. With his mind free of worry over finding Alice again, he started working on the problem of getting into the compound. When he and Alice witnessed the brawl at the entrance, he recalled that the gates remained open for truck traffic, but no posted guards.

Weary from the long walk, Kurt expected to see the smoke by now, but the sky was dark, muddled by low clouds. Even the odor of the place was gone. He hoped he wasn't lost. There was no racket of trucks or buses. He scanned the black woods, his eyes finally snagging on a nearly imperceptible smudge of light beyond the tangle of limbs and leaves. It had to be the compound.

When he reached the perimeter fencing, he headed in the direction of the gate he and Alice had seen. What was the plan? To enter and hope no one paid attention to him? From what he recalled, everyone was either dressed in blue coveralls, or wearing all black like the guards, with intimidating helmets and dark visors. No way could he enter unnoticed.

Less than a couple hundred feet from the opened gates, Kurt watched from the thick underbrush. Everything was quiet; no one milling about, no trucks or buses. The compound, which had bustled with violence and activity several hours earlier, now appeared deserted.

Everyone left and didn't bother to lock the gates? That seemed odd.

Kurt eased out from the thicket toward the compound, his head shifting side to side. Every so often he'd stop and listen; the only sound returning; that of the leaves rustling behind him under a steady breeze.

Huge overhead flood lights painted the grounds and parking lot around the austere five-story building in a stark, frigid light. Many of the windows glowed dull yellow or green, but not a soul anywhere that Kurt could see. He paused at the entrance to the building, the sign above reading:

OTTO PLASTICS AND INJECTION MOLDING—SITE 13

Kurt grabbed the handles of the double metal doors, expecting them to be locked when he jerked back. When they opened unexpectedly, it caused him to lose his balance for a moment. Inside was a wide, well-lit corridor with doors along both sides, and a stairwell in the center leading up to an open atrium. Kurt spied a pair of elevators beyond the staircase and chose to explore those. The place looked deserted, the only sound that of dripping water echoing through the void.

He had just pushed the up arrow when he heard muffled voices coming from behind the elevator doors, descending toward him. The murmuring grew louder, more distinct, followed by excited laughter, the elevator humming to a stop. Kurt dashed down a side corridor and ducked into an open office just as the elevator doors opened.

The voices floated down the hall. Two men, it sounded like. Kurt pictured them as guards, wearing all black, with some kind of batons, remembering back to the brawl at the gate, the batons capable of incapacitating grown men. Maybe the batons functioned like cattle prods, powerful enough to lay a person out cold.

The men sounded close. Just outside the open door now, Kurt was able to catch snatches of conversation. One of them mentioned *scrams*—a term Kurt had never heard— saying that they'd had an uptick of violent situations lately at the plant, the scrams more erratic than usual.

"I think it's Leviathan," the other man said, "that's got 'em in a frenzy, the brainless bastards."

The first man laughed. "I don't think those crazy fucks even know what Leviathan is!"

Kurt smelled cigarette smoke as the men talked.

"Maybe they sense the impending doom..." the other man said, chortling. "What do I know."

"Is it true the AP is leaving them in the housing buildings?"

"That's what I heard. Kind of cruel, if you ask me, but there's only so much room up there...and they're...well, they're scrams...screwed from the get-go, the sad assholes."

"When do you ship out?"

"Early next week."

"That's cutting it close, don't you think?"

"Naw...I'm still not convinced the damn thing's even gonna hit. Forty-seven percent chance, I think, at last estimate."

A short interlude of silence followed until one of the men said, "I have to check the manufacturing floors, then head over to C Building and make sure they have all the machinery turned off. Not that it will matter much once we cut the power."

"I hear you. Shutting this plant down seems pointless if you ask me." The man laughed. "In two weeks it may not even be here!"

"Take care!"

"You too, Hobbes."

Footfalls echoed down the hallway as fluorescent lights stuttered on above Kurt's head, buzzing like enormous bees in the medium-sized office, light flying everywhere. Kurt tucked deeper under the desk, but the space was too cramped to hold his entire frame. A few seconds later the lights shut off, the sudden darkness a relief.

The man departed the office, leaving a trail of his own loud footfalls reporting back like gunfire at first, then fading to muffled thumps, then gone. Kurt held his position, adjusting it slightly to give himself a bit more room.

After a few minutes of silence, Kurt got up and rubbed the stiffness from his legs, then peeked out the doorway.

The hallway was clear, the fluorescent tubes glowing, droning along the ceiling, a sound that would largely go unnoticed except in this hushed void. Kurt headed for the illuminated exit sign above the door at the end of the hallway. Taking the stairs seemed less risky than riding the noisy elevator.

The concrete stairwell took Kurt to the second floor, where he carefully opened the door, giving him a direct view of an empty gangway. The door on the third-floor landing, however, opened into a vast, dark space filled with all kinds of machinery. A high, shadowy ceiling—crisscrossed with girders, pipes, valves, and conduits—stretched across the open space, with rectangular fluorescent work lights hanging by wires at regular intervals ten feet above the stained concrete floor.

This was the place Kurt was hoping to find. Colored lights glowed from the back corner of the factory. Kurt moved slowly through the labyrinth of dormant machines and devices, the caustic stink of oil, plastic and solvents fouling the air. Though he hadn't put eyes on them yet, he knew he wasn't far from the vending machines, the red and blue lights shining brighter toward the back.

Before he reached the machines, he heard talking. And applause. He crouched down next to a large machine and listened, unsure if he could trust his ears. The Ed Sullivan Show? He recognized the music, then Ed Sullivan introducing Peter, Paul and Mary, the famous folk group, followed by thunderous applause from the television speaker. Barely had the trio started singing their most recent number one hit, "I Dig Rock and Roll Music," when all sound ended abruptly, followed by a thick silence.

A few seconds later, one of the vending machines came to life, the interior mechanism shattering the quiet, its inner workings delivering its payload under a metallic clatter. Kurt froze, picturing a hand reaching down into the open trough to retrieve the cold, brightly-labeled can.

A moment later, the hush was interrupted again by the unmistakable pop and pressure release of a pull tab. Kurt figured it must be the guard who was going to check on the machinery.

"Ugh, that's disgusting!" the man shouted. The can flew across the space, crashing against the far wall. "How can scrams drink that shit!"

Kurt cowered lower behind the grease-stained plastic injection mold machine; the device evidently manufactured by Howell according to the metal label riveted to the housing. The guard walked past Kurt's position, stopping briefly by the Howell machine.

"Who's there?" the man said, then waited a moment before he added, "Is someone there?"

Kurt stopped his breathing, while his heart was a galloping mess.

Chapter Eleven

Kurt didn't know how long he could hold his breath. The man was apparently still standing a few yards away, waiting, though Kurt couldn't see him.

"I can smell you," the man said. "I know you're there."

Smell me? Kurt quietly sniffed near his armpit. It was certainly possible, as much as Kurt had been sweating over the past couple of days trudging through the woods. But the slight bit of body odor he detected didn't seem enough for someone to pick up from twelve feet away.

"You know I can smell you scrams! Now get your ass out here."

Kurt edged slowly around the machine until he could lay eyes on the man, unable to believe he could possibly smell him above the stench of motor lubricants and burned plastic. When Kurt finally spied the guard, he saw that the man was facing away from the Howell injection mold machine, shouting at some other machine across the aisle.

The guard started laughing. "Stinking scrams," he said, moving off toward the entrance to the factory floor. "I can smell all you stinking scrams, your sweat on the machines, your stink in the air!" he shouted, then laughed. "It oozes out of your pores!" A minute or so later, the lights hanging from the ceiling started snapping off until the space was cast into near total darkness, the glow from the vending machines and exit signs the only light remaining.

After the guard departed, Kurt hurried over and stood before the vending machines, eyeing the candy bars, the chips, the soda labels. He had no money, and though he had never stolen anything in his life until two days ago, he now seemed capable of stealing anything in sight. Tonight would be no different.

Searching near the plastic injection devices, he found a huge wrench and carried it over to the vending machines, then smashed the glass and grabbed all the candy bars, setting them on a chair. Hershey's, 100 Grand Bar, Mars, Milk Duds, Good & Plenty. Then the chip machine; bags of Fritos, Potato Chips, Bugles and Doritos scattered across the floor. He pounded on the Coke machine until the door came open, then grabbed two cans of cold Coke, sliding one down into each front pants pocket. He found a plain cardboard box of worn-out parts sitting by the trash can and dumped them out on the floor, quickly filling the box with all the food he'd pilfered from the machines.

"I'm sorry," he said into the empty air, knowing someone would have to pay for everything he'd broken and taken. He walked to the factory floor entrance, careful not to trip on anything in the dark, then carried his box to the stairwell and hurried down to the first floor.

The building was darker now, the main lights extinguished. The emergency lighting provided the only illumination to the exits. He stepped from the building, the box under his arm, the soda cans pulling down on his trousers, and was about to walk toward the gates when a car raced around the corner from the back of the building, the headlights cutting an eerie path toward the gate. Kurt fell back against the building, into the shadows.

The driver was just about out of the front gate when a

man in blue coveralls stepped in front of the vehicle. The car never even slowed down, running the man over, then racing away in a stream of dust.

Kurt was dumbfounded, unable to parse the savagery of the event. Even worse, the man lying on the ground appeared to still be alive. Kurt walked near him, unable to look at him, his blue coveralls blossoming with blood. "Help," the man said, blood bubbling from his mouth when he spoke. "Help. Help me."

Unable to do anything for the injured man, Kurt gave him wide berth, then hurried through the front gates and made a beeline for the woods. He felt terrible leaving the man to suffer, and probably die, but convinced himself that Alice was his first priority. He had to stay focused, had to get back to her. Relieved to find the first strand of gauze, he followed the trail all the way back to the clearing, happy that the plan had worked.

But Alice was gone.

Chapter Twelve

"Alice!" he called. "Alice, where are you?" The day was aging slowly, spreading brilliant yellow light up beyond the web of trees and limbs and leaves. "Alice!"

"I'm here, Kurt," she said, ambling out from the dense vegetation. "I had to go to the bathroom."

"Alice! I thought something happened to you."

"I saw your note…and started to follow the markers, then just came back and waited. Like you told me." Alice walked over to the slab rock where Kurt had set down the box of food. She picked up one of the candy bars and smelled it. "The gauze was a great idea, Kurt. You're very resourceful."

Something was off. Alice wasn't herself, her tone uncharacteristically flat and disinterested, as if she'd been drained of all life, neither scared, nor pleased. Nothing. She sat on the rock with the box in her lap and opened the bag of Fritos.

He fished a red soda can out of one of his front pockets, then the second from the other. He opened Alice's and handed it to her, then sat down and opened his. They chewed in silence, his mind swirled with problematic images, words that made no sense; *Leviathan. Scrams.* Meaningless, foreign terms with potentially devastating significance. He forced his eyes open, until they burned unmercifully. He allowed them to close, and the movie playing inside his head fed a bleak and savage world—a deep-red montage filled with screaming and shouting; a dog's severed head spinning through the air; a body broken and pleading for help; blood bubbling from parted lips; the bloody exposed bone of an unrecognizable skull smashed to pulp; the flash of a shiny blade slicing flesh; fighting; cursing; fists smashing into faces; the cruel sound of breaking bones; the stench of death, fire, wreckage; bus windows blurring by, filled with pale, hopeless faces; the black pungent smoke of burning tires and oil; a man's detached metallic head dripping fluids; a shotgun blast ripping through wood, over and over and over; the stink of burnt gunpowder; the reek of cigarette smoke.

Kurt couldn't halt the parade of sounds and smells and gruesome memories.

"I have to sleep, Alice," he said, setting down his soda can, then crumpling to the ground.

WHEN KURT WOKE, his mouth was so dry it hurt. He tried activating his salivary glands by running his tongue along the inside of his mouth. Useless. He gently sucked, hoping to get the fluids moving. A squirrel chattered in a tree nearby. Eventually he heard the birds chirping and realized where he was.

Somewhere in the woods.

Nowhere, really.

Alice?

He stretched his neck, then got up on one elbow, swiveling his head to find her. His neck was stiff again. He sat up and reached around behind him to grab the soda can. It was warm. He drank it anyway, sloshing it around in his mouth. The box of food was gone. Which didn't matter; he wasn't hungry.

"Alice?" he called. The sky was gray, spitting rain, the branches above clattering against one another by the hand of the wind. Trying to get to his feet, he collapsed back down, his legs too wobbly to stand. Getting older was getting harder, and living on the lam didn't help.

Eventually he got to his hands and knees, then finally stood upright. Alice appeared, carrying the box with the snacks. "You're up," she said, setting the box down on the rock.

"I guess it doesn't matter what time it is…" Kurt said, making conversation, wondering how she was doing, where she'd been. "But it'd be nice to know, right?"

"I hope you weren't hungry," she said without looking at him. "I took the box with me to keep the critters out."

He nodded, stirring his hand through the chips, finding the bag of Doritos. "Want to share?" He held the bag out to her while opening it.

"I don't want any." She seemed pensive.

"Where were you?" Kurt asked.

"I followed the gauze markers back to the compound."

Panic shot through him. "Why!"

"I don't know, Kurt…" Her eyes appeared to be swelling, until the tears came, just a drop or two at first, until they streamed down her cheeks. "That man killed Bella like she was nothing, like her life didn't matter!" Alice sniffled, wiping under her nose with her wrist. "Then I…then I killed that man like he was nothing, Kurt," Alice said, her eyes scorched red, her hand up at her mouth. "I killed him like his life didn't matter…"

The tears came in waves now, her body heaving.

He came over and put his arm around her. "Please, don't Alice. You saved our lives. You didn't do anything wrong."

"How can you say that, Kurt! I killed a man! How is that even possible!"

Kurt's mind retraced the events from the previous evening, the guards talking about scrams; *well, shit, they're scrams…screwed from the get go, the sad assholes.* Was the man that Alice killed a scram? Was there something different about scrams? The guard near the vending machines going on about scrams, screaming at shadows like a lunatic; *I can smell all you stinking scrams, your sweat on the machines, your stink in the air!* Kurt remembered when the man with the machete first approached him and Alice. Kurt could tell something was off about him, nothing noticeable or glaringly obvious, but maybe a dozen subtle details that Kurt's conscious mind couldn't make sense of, while his instincts could.

Alice was pulling herself together, sniffling, wiping her eyes. "What are we going to do?"

Kurt didn't know, but he didn't want to send her a message of hopelessness. "How did the compound look when you got there?"

She brought her eyes to his. "Deserted. But there was…"

"What?"

"A man in blue coveralls lying in the dirt near the front gates…. He was dead, Kurt. His clothes covered in blood."

Kurt didn't want to scare her by telling her he'd seen the car that ran the man over, not even slowing down or attempting to stop. Kurt just nodded. Alice's expression turned gloomy, but she let the subject drop, as if she knew that Kurt had already seen the man himself.

A light drizzle wet the dirt, along with their snack bags and candy bars. A second later, a bright flash burned the woods white for a moment, followed by a booming thunder clap. The rain came harder, quickly soaking them both.

"Let's go back," Kurt said, figuring the factory was

deserted now. "Get out of this rain. We can regroup…make a plan. Maybe find a change of clothes or something."

Alice was in agreement, picking up the box of snacks.

They followed the gauze strips back to the compound, Kurt pushing aside limbs for Alice. The green sky cut loose, the rain a deluge by the time they reached the compound. Kurt dashed through the open gates for the double doors, avoiding the dead man in the mud, Alice on his heels.

Once inside, they wiped the water from their hair, both of them chilled. The exit signs, and emergency lighting, had gone dark, the batteries obviously dead. Plenty of diffuse light from the windows illuminated the facility, at least until night came. They'd be gone by then.

Kurt led her to the stairwell and up to the fourth floor, hoping to find more vending machines—ones he hadn't already pillaged—and maybe a restroom with showers and lockers, and possibly even dry clothes.

The pungent stink of industrial grime, electrical wiring, lubricants and oxidizing metal filled their senses when they entered the machine-choked space. Kurt was relieved to see the light coming through the banks of high windows. The sky outside the factory was green, rain slashing at the window panes. Like the level Kurt had visited the evening before, this one also hosted high ceilings strewn with a convoluted network of metal trusses, pipes, conduits and a grid work of pipes forming a sprinkler system. At the far end, stood two freight elevators, which might be situated near a few vending machines and maybe a break room.

Electricity no longer flowed to the vending machines; the front panels dark. Kurt found a hammer and pounded on the door of the soda machine until it popped open. The cans were still cold. "Come pick what you want, Alice."

Alice withdrew a 7Up and popped the tab, taking a long drink. Kurt opted for an RC Cola. When he went to check the snack machines to see what they offered, he told Alice he found her favorite, Mr. Goodbar. She was gone. Just then she called to him, her voice muffled.

"Where are you?" he called.

"In here!"

He followed her voice to a door with a sign that read, LADIES. He opened it slowly. "Alice?" he called again, as if it might be inhabited by other women, which was crazy. When he penetrated deeper, the main door easing closed behind him, he heard the sound of a functioning shower. "Alice?"

"Hurry, Kurt. Grab one before the water runs out."

He saw her clothes in a heap on the floor, quickly finding the stall next to hers. Within seconds he was luxuriating under a warm shower, utilizing the smooth remains of a bar of soap. He lathered his hair, under his arms, his legs, moving with haste before the water ran cold, or out completely.

"This is amazing!" Alice said.

"Unbelievable!"

Kurt turned his faucet off, and proceeded to pull open locker doors, looking for a couple of towels. In the corner he saw a wire mesh trash can half-filled with white towels. He reached down into it, checking to see if they were wet. They weren't. He pulled two out, and asked Alice if she was opposed to a pre-used towel.

"No clean ones?"

"No!" Did she think they were at the Howard Johnsons?

"Okay, then..." Her hand came out from the shower curtain. "It's starting to run cold."

He pushed the towel into her open palm.

"Thanks, Kurt." Her water shut off, but she stayed behind the curtain.

Kurt wrapped his towel around his waist and started checking lockers for dry clothes. Any clothes. Something other than the filthy rags they were wearing. He checked at least ten lockers—opening the flimsy doors, then banging them closed—before he came across a set of folded blue coveralls on the upper shelf. He held them up; far too small for him but looked like they'd fit Alice.

"I set some fresh clothes on the bench here," he called to Alice. "I'm gonna check the men's locker room."

"Thanks. I'll be out in a minute."

He went down the line of lockers, checking each one until he found blue coveralls hanging on the hook. The garment was oil-stained, one ripped sleeve with what looked like dried blood. He continued his search, finally coming upon coveralls that not only appeared clean, but might actually fit him. He unfurled them, stepped into the legs and brought the top up over his shoulders. The pant legs were a little short, but at least they fit loosely in the crotch, and just a bit snug in the shoulders, but tolerable.

He found a pair of work socks that looked practically new, then went back to see how Alice was coming along. She stood in bare feet before the full-length mirror modeling her coveralls. They looked like they fit her well. She looked over at him, her eyes dropping to his socks. "Wow, where did you find those?"

"Next door," he said, signaling with a thumb over his shoulder. "Only one pair. You want 'em?" He sat on the bench to take them off.

"No, you keep them. Mine aren't too bad."

She sat next to him, fishing her dirty socks and wet shoes from her pile of clothes. Kurt found his wet shoes and hated putting them on over his new, dry socks.

"How's the wound doing?" he asked.

"It's fine. A little red, but it doesn't hurt. The floss is holding up well."

He nodded, glad it wasn't infected.

Finished dressing, they went back out to the vending machines. Kurt walked down the line, using the hammer to break the glass on each machine. Alice picked out a few items she wanted, then seated herself at one of the tables in the adjoining break room.

Kurt ambled over with his bounty, paying special attention to the time punch clock, the rack of cards attached to the wall next to it. He'd never worked a job where he'd had to punch in and out, but Alice had at the hardware store. Near the punch clock hung a new 1967 Chevrolet calendar with photos of all the latest models of automobiles. Kurt figured the plastics plant made parts for the car manufacturer. He flipped back to the cover, to a sleek blue Stingray Corvette. Thumbing through the months, he marveled at all the sparkling new cars, repeating the names in his head; Bel Air, Biscayne, Caprice, Impala, Chevelle, Chevy Nova, a gold Camaro, the rear-engine Corvair and others. On the last page was a picture of an El Camino coupe utility vehicle sitting on a beach at sunset. Reed would have gone crazy for these cars. Well, maybe not the Corvair, so much.

"I feel almost human again," Alice said, chewing on a bite of her Mr. Goodbar when Kurt entered the break room. Lying next to her on the table was an unopened bag of Fritos.

"The shower was incredible," he said, ripping open his bag of Bugles. His mind was still on Reed and the cars. "Reed would have been twenty-two years old soon."

Alice, without looking over at him, nodded in the affirmative. "In a couple of weeks from now," she said, suddenly curious. "Why do you ask?"

"Do you think he'd be married now?"

Alice smiled, chuckling. "I think he'd be in college, and…maybe have a special girl. He really wanted to be a mechanical engineer, remember? He loved figuring out how things worked."

Kurt remembered now, Reed taking his toy train engine apart to see what was inside, captivated by all the little plastic gears and the electric motor. He was even able to put it back together and make it work again, as Kurt recalled.

"What made you think about that?" Alice asked, looking over at him.

Kurt started explaining about the calendar, and all the new cars, then Reed's birthday, when he looked over at Alice. She was glaring at him, setting her candy bar on the table. Her features had soured, as if she were about to be sick, her hand covering her mouth.

"What's wrong?" Kurt asked.

"The coveralls you're wearing…they remind me of…of…"

"Hey, let's put all that behind us and start over, okay…"

"He's still there…"

"Who? Where?"

"The man I killed. They just left him under the fence, his head…"

She was sobbing, rocking back and forth.

"Who broke those machines?" a voice said, interrupting their conversation.

Kurt swung around, jumping to his feet. Alice froze, her eyes fixed on the intruders. Three strangers in blue coveralls; two men, one woman.

Chapter Thirteen

"Did you break them?" the tall, balding man asked.

"We found them that way," Kurt said, eyeing the hammer twelve feet away on the floor, amidst all the broken glass.

"They weren't broken yesterday morning," the man with the beard said. His glasses were outfitted with thick lenses, making his pupils appear owl-like. But it wasn't just the glasses, Kurt realized; they all had dilated pupils, as if they'd just come from the eye doctor.

"They weren't," the woman said. "I know because I put my money in that one." She pointed at the soda machine. "I had a Dr Pepper. Dr Pepper is my favorite." She gave Alice a broken-smile, her teeth a yellow jagged fence.

"Somebody will have to pay for that," the man with the beard said. He adjusted his glasses, blinking several times before his eyebrows rose comically, like a facial tic.

"That's for sure," Kurt said.

"Do you work here?" the tall, balding man asked. "I've never seen you before."

"My name is Betty," the woman said, grinning, her pronouncement aimed at Alice. "What's yours?"

"Alice."

"That's a pretty name. Alice. Alice. Alice in Wonderland."

The men chuckled at Betty's comment. The bearded man with thick glasses repeated it. "Alice in Wonderland." He smiled at his own remark, then turned instantly grim. "You don't look like Alice in Wonderland."

A sudden flash of lightning interrupted the exchange, followed by a clap of thunder that shook the glass in all the windows. The tall balding man screamed, which caused the woman to rush Alice, knocking her to the floor, both of them tangled together. Alice wrapped her arms over her head to protect herself. Kurt rushed over to pull the woman off Alice when the man with the thick glasses shouted, "NO!" threatening Kurt with the hammer he'd picked up. Kurt ignored the man, pulling Betty off Alice. Betty started screaming, jumping up and down, then running through the broken glass, pulling the snacks from the machines and throwing them to the floor, cutting her arms in the process. Another flash of lightning, and the immediate crack of thunder sent the balding man running wildly, screaming, his hands covering his ears. Blood ran down both of Betty's arms, from her elbows to her wrists. When the man with the glasses saw the blood, he ran to Betty and smashed her head over and over with the hammer until Betty was a lifeless lump amongst the broken glass and blood. The balding man hurried away, dodging through the machinery on the factory floor until he was gone.

The man with the hammer stared at Kurt.

"I should kill you for what you did to Betty!" He sneered, eyes blinking. His eyebrows jerked upwards with a comical cadence, but there was nothing funny about the intensity he aimed at Kurt. Without warning, he charged Kurt, who easily side-stepped him, using the man's momentum to toss him toward the tables and chairs. The man stumbled awkwardly, unable to keep his feet beneath him, crying and shouting as he slammed to the floor. The hammer spun across the dirty concrete, slamming into the back wall. Kurt hurried over to retrieve the weapon before the man could regain his footing, then spun around, expecting to thwart an attack, when he stepped on something that crunched beneath his shoe. The man's glasses. Kurt looked at the broken specs, then took his eyes to the man, who hadn't moved, his body tangled in the upturned chairs.

Alice stood back, her arms wrapping her body.

Kurt eased over toward him, with the hammer raised above his head.

"Be careful, Kurt," she said.

He nodded, squatting just enough to reach out to the man's wrist to check for a pulse.

"He's dead," Kurt said, confused. How could he be dead? He barely fell, and broke his fall with his hands. Kurt was fairly certain the man never even hit his head. There was no blood.

"Let's get out of here, Kurt. I'm scared."

Kurt nodded, his attention drawn to the downpour outside the factory windows, the rain so dense it appeared as a solid sheet of gray. Kurt dropped the hammer, glancing toward the vending machines, and Betty's lifeless body, his eyes focused on her bloody, ruined face.

"Yeah, let's get out of here," Kurt said.

Using the stairwell, they stepped quietly down the concrete steps to the first floor in case anyone else had come to the compound. Kurt still couldn't understand what those people were doing here. The plant was closed down, the electricity shut off; the guards he'd overheard had been very clear about that.

Kurt and Alice searched the offices and storage areas on the first floor, Kurt believing the plant had to have some kind of rainwear, or at least jackets, for the maintenance staff and guards. Alice found a large metal locker near the entrance with safety vests and rainwear. They grabbed rain jackets with hoods, then hurried from the building in the rain. They crossed the parking lot and fled through the huge double gates. They had not formulated a plan, but at least they had clean dry clothes for now, protected from the rain. Through some unspoken agreement, they would process the horrific events of a half hour earlier separately, privately, at some point in the future. Most importantly now was to get as far from the plastics plant as possible.

Chapter Fourteen

When would this nightmare end?

After fleeing through the front gates, they followed the muddy road leading away from the plastics plant. Alice agreed that following the road was their best chance of finding a town or city. There was only one problem, which Kurt kept to himself; based on his own observations, Kurt worried about the amount of truck and bus traffic traveling the route. Of course, that was before the plant shut down. The road was also secluded, and rough—certainly not a main thoroughfare—with forest on either side that would provide quick cover if a vehicle happened by. While their main objective was finding a small town or city, they certainly didn't want to come face to face with more people like Betty and her clan.

Scrams. That's what Kurt figured them for, whatever that moniker meant. Kurt was familiar with the outmoded word, *scram,* a slang word meaning, *get out of here.* But in the context of a group classification of people, it made no sense.

The storm was easing as they traversed the mucky rutted road away from the Otto plastics plant, but the overcast sky would make it impossible to know when night was approaching. Kurt recalled the time punch clock near the locker rooms; the hands at two-thirty-eight. But that was at least an hour ago, or longer. The calculation was unreliable. He just hoped they'd find a safe haven before dark.

Just as they crested a slight rise in the road, a group of people walking in the opposite direction approached, all clothed in blue coveralls. An audible, "Oh, no!" escaped Alice's lips. Kurt turned back toward her briefly, telling her to follow his lead, that they would be fine.

"Just keep your head down," he said.

"Hi!" one of them said. "I'm Byron. I work at the Otto plastics plant. Do you work there?"

Kurt nodded without stopping. "Yes," he said, "we just finished our shift."

"Did they reopen the plant?" one of them shouted, the group stopping to hear the answer.

"Yes. Hobbes," Kurt said, recalling the name of the guard he'd overheard, "said everything's back to normal."

"Yay," they said in unison, congratulating one another, smiling.

"Calvin is a good guy," one of them said. "His name is Calvin Hobbes. He's a good guy."

The group turned, laughing and talking, and continued on toward the plant.

Alice caught up to Kurt. "They're gonna know you lied when they get there…"

Kurt spun toward her. "So, what!" he shouted, quietly. "There's something wrong with these people, okay? Let's just keep moving!"

"They're going to find those bodies—"

"I don't give a shit what they find! I've had it with all this crap! I'm at the end of my fucking rope, here, Alice!" Kurt's breath rose and fell, his heart clattering.

She stepped back, putting space between them, her jaw

tightening. Her head began to bob, as if nodding. "I'm sorry, Kurt. I know you don't mean to be short with me. And—"

He reached out and pulled her to him. "I'm so sorry, Alice! I'm just...I don't know...It's just..."

She tightened her arms around him. "It's okay. Let's just keep moving."

"I love you, Alice," he said, not ready to let her go.

"I love you, too."

They kissed briefly, then continued up the road, Alice following a few steps behind.

A short while later, they passed more scrams in their signature blue coveralls, like a work-detail from a prison, Kurt shamelessly prevaricating, the scrams none the wiser. If anything, the motley bunch had left more hopeful, happier than they'd been only moments before they met Kurt and Alice.

Kurt hadn't expected to meet scrams along the road, wondering why they would be walking to the plant if it was closed? Maybe they weren't told, the guards wishing to avoid bizarre scenes like the one he and Alice had witnessed. But the scrams would give them cover if a car went by. Apparently scrams walked this road all the time, so Kurt and Alice wouldn't look out of place. But why were they walking to the plant? Were these routine trips to use the showers, or vending machines, or toilets? Or maybe they felt at home around the machinery. Who knew where they lived, or how? And what about the ones he'd seen being driven from the plant aboard blue buses? Did they live farther than the ones he and Alice passed on the road? Did scrams live anywhere, have homes or apartments? Or were they just nomads, wanderers, their minds too far gone to know any different? Kurt couldn't believe he was capable of classifying an entire group of people with such cruelty, believing scrams were incapable of normal social interaction—taking care of a home, of themselves—a prejudice Kurt had never before felt, had never known existed within himself.

It was mind boggling.

The past few days had been surreal, and Kurt felt himself losing cohesion in his own reality.

They walked on, passing more scrams, Kurt repeating the lies, both of them keeping to themselves, until Kurt looked up and noticed the sky was dark. He couldn't recall when that had happened, so focused on the road, the scrams, and the otherworldliness of their situation.

"Can we rest, Kurt?" Alice said. "I need to stop for a spell."

"Sure," Kurt said, looking for a place to sit. Up ahead, no more than fifty yards or so, he spied something that looked like bus stops on either side of the crappy road. "Can you make it to those shelters?"

"Absolutely."

They picked up their pace, relieved to be able to sit on actual benches. The lighting made them feel safe. The little shelters appeared surprisingly clean, except for some dust from the road that had settled on the window frames. They hadn't even bothered wiping down the seats, too weary to care about dirt anymore.

Alice brought out a fresh Mr. Goodbar from her upper pocket. She ripped the top open and handed it to Kurt. He took a bite, then handed it back. They passed it between them until it was gone. Alice got up, deposited the wrapper in the lidded trash can next to the shelter, then sat back down next to Kurt and started crying, her face in her hands.

"What's wrong, Alice?"

She sniffed, bringing her head up, then wiping her tears. "I don't know," she said, then started laughing, sniffling again, wiping the rest of her tears with her hand. "I think I'm losing my mind…and it feels pretty good…"

Kurt started laughing, both of them wiping their tears.

Just then headlights came toward them on the opposite side of the road. It was a blue bus headed for the Otto plant. The driver stopped and opened his window. "You heading back to the barracks?"

"No," Kurt said. "We're going that way." Kurt pointed down the road away from the plant, trying to respond the way a scram might.

The driver appeared perplexed by Kurt's answer. "I know you're going that way," he said, his statement terse. "You're waiting in the westbound shelter…"

"How could you know?" Kurt asked, trying to match a scram's flat aspect. "We didn't tell you."

"Aw, fuck it," the driver said, shaking his head. The bus rolled slightly backward as the driver eased off the brake, then quickly lurched forward when he let the clutch out. "You morons are on your own!" He stuck his fist out the window, middle finger raised, as he drove off.

"I think you made a new friend, Kurt," Alice said, both of them watching the red taillights burn a path through the night.

Kurt stood up, offering his hand to Alice. "To the barracks?"

"Not if our luck holds," Alice said.

They walked on, the evening turning cooler, a steady breeze coming from the north. Kurt feared another bout of rain was headed their way, or worse, another storm. He kept his eyes to the woods on both sides of the road, hoping to find a clearing or shelter. Not far in the distance, the road seemed to be interrupted by a bridge. Cover and water, if their *luck held,* according to Alice. He'd been buoyed by her joke, and the irony; with all that had happened she hadn't lost her sense of humor.

When they reached the bridge, they scrambled down the dark embankment only to find railroad tracks, the smell of creosote burning in Kurt's nostrils. "Have you ever hopped a train, Alice?"

"I may not possess the skills of a seasoned hobo, but I'm pretty sure I smell like one!"

Kurt sat a moment. Even though they had left the bus shelter a short while ago, fatigue was overtaking him, both physical and mental.

Alice started up the steep embankment.

"Wait, where you going?" Kurt said, unable to get up just yet.

"I heard something," she said, disappearing from sight up the hill.

Kurt listened, the sickly, oily stink of creosote making him nauseous.

"Kurt, come here!" Alice called, her voice sounding distant.

Kurt pushed himself up, his legs stiff, his feet aching. He trudged up the hill, grabbing saplings to haul himself up the steep incline. Reaching the top, he noticed Alice on the far side of the road, looking down into the valley. "Is it Rescue?" he said, using up his last shred of humor.

"No," she said, chuckling. "But close."

He walked over and stood next to her, letting his eyes find what she was seeing. Lights. Enough for a town or small city, with more lights in the distance. Civilization.

Chapter Fifteen

The hike down to the main highway took almost six hours.

During that lengthy journey, they had passed *the barracks*, a dismal array of corrugated metal buildings with semi-circle-roofed Quonset huts arranged in military rows. In the parking lot just beyond the buildings, beneath a grid of floodlights, sat a row of blue buses.

Kurt and Alice eventually came to a paved two-lane highway with no traffic. They walked along it for quite a long time—heading in the direction of the town Alice had spotted—when they happened upon a rustic rest area, with little parking and no vehicles. Near the wooden building with a sagging roof stood a fifteen-foot telephone pole with a rusty floodlight attached, the dim illumination dying out before it reached the far edges of the lot.

They figured the rest stop was abandoned, and never expected to find the bathrooms unlocked. Especially surprising was the fact that the water was still on. They washed their hands and face, ate the chips they'd stolen at the plant, then found a picnic table away from the light they could sleep on.

Kurt told Alice to take the top, that he'd sleep on the seat. They argued a bit, until Kurt crawled up on top, and Alice stretched out on the seat below him. It seemed they had just said goodnight when it started to pour. They rushed inside the dilapidated restrooms and tried to get comfortable on the filthy concrete floor. Exhausted, they both slept until daylight filled the small building.

They got up, used the toilets, had a snack, drank from the faucets, then headed up the highway, walking the last three hours of their nine-hour trek from the Otto plant to the city limits.

The metal sign read:

Ottomon. Population 2,146

"Ottomon? Isn't that about 200 miles north of Rescue?" Kurt asked.

"I believe so..." Alice said. "We're not that far from home."

"Rescue has over 3000 people, right?"

"Why?" she said.

"Perspective, I guess. I'm trying to manage expectations about Ottomon..."

"Go ahead and splurge, Kurt! Go crazy. Expect whatever you want. Who knows...we might be home soon!"

They started walking down the hill toward the row of buildings lining the main street through Ottomon. Trying to ward off disappointment, Kurt pushed away the impression that the town was as deserted as the rustic rest area had been. Parking meters lined the street like useless sentries, with less than four automobiles situated along the curb. Five if you counted the beat up old pickup truck parked, or abandoned, at the corner. No pedestrians on the sidewalks, or milling about as far as they could see. Most of the storefronts were dark, closed signs in the windows. Maybe it was Sunday. There was no way to know, time now more of a luxury than a given.

Despite the absence of activity, the aroma of cooked food was unmistakable. Kurt kept his nose tuned as they traversed the sleepy town, the sky growing darker, greener, the wind swirling loose trash along the gutters and down the street. Huge drops of rain splashed on the hood and windshield of an older model white and turquoise DeSoto, when the sky cut loose, drowning everything under a gray sheet of water. Kurt and Alice stayed close to the storefronts, scurrying beneath the awnings and overhangs, when they came to a diner.

Without hesitation, they pushed through the screen door, into a long rectangular room running front to back. To their left, occupying nearly the entire length of the wall, was a full bar stocked with colorful bottles in front of a huge mirror. Down the center of the establishment sat a series of round tables, four chairs each, and a pool table in the back, the green felt alive with light from the fixture hanging above it. Just beyond the pool table, a sign marking restrooms, Ladies and Gents.

A few patrons sat at the tables, drinking beer and eating, with five or so men standing or sitting on red barstools talking, laughing, and smoking. In fact, as Kurt's eyes roved the poorly lit space, he noticed everyone was smoking, the air near the stamped-metal ceiling clouded with smoke.

It took less than ten seconds for the bartender to take notice of their presence. His face darkened and with a huff, he threw his bar towel into the sink and aimed his hairy arm toward the front entrance, his first finger pointing, leaving little doubt as to his state of mind. "You know you can't come in here!" he screamed. "So, *scram!*" He paused a second, his comrades around the bar breaking into a huge belly laugh, the bartender nearly choking with amusement at his harsh pun.

Kurt and Alice stood dumbstruck, unmoving, water dripping onto the floor. The bartender's face turned red. He became animated, waving his fist at them. "Did you fucking hear me? *SCRAM!*"

The rest of the bar clan laughed again, but the bartender didn't join in this time, his eyes like razor blades on Kurt and Alice. An older couple eating their food ignored the entire scene with such purpose and determination, they seemed almost absurd in their denial of what was happening.

How could anyone hate with that much verve at merely the sight of someone? Kurt thought back to his own revulsion over the scrams, how quickly he'd lost patience with their idiocy.

"We're sorry," Kurt said, trying not to anger the man any further. "We just need help."

The bartender hurried toward the end of the bar and started to raise the flapper door, as if about to physically dislodge them, then held it steady.

"Get out of my tavern!" the man shouted.

No one was laughing now.

"Come on, Kurt," Alice whispered. "Let's go." She tugged on the back of his coveralls.

Kurt was as big as the bartender, maybe bigger, which may have been the reason the bartender thought better of moving the confrontation beyond the threat stage, making it a little *too real* if flesh and bone became involved.

"We just need some damn help, mister." Kurt was emboldened by the bartender's hesitancy. All eyes shifted to the bartender now, except for the couple eating, who quickly downed their iced teas and wiped their mouths.

"I know you need *help*, scram, but you came to the wrong damn place. Go down to the Blue-Plate Special. They serve your kind down there!"

"Look mister," Kurt started to say, when a woman sitting at the table nearest to them, said in a quiet voice that maybe they should just go. Kurt hadn't noticed her before, too busy sizing up the rest of the room. She was young, mid-thirties, with dark hair. Attractive by any standard. The man with her was a dapper fella, about her age. The only difference between the two of them was that he was minding his own business, and she wasn't.

"Just shut up, lady," Kurt said, surprised by his own callousness, though unable to check himself. "You have no fucking idea what we've been through!"

"Kurt!" Alice said, clearly shocked.

Kurt glanced toward Alice, his expression stern, then glared down at the nosey young woman, then at her man, who seemed to want nothing to do with the impending fracas. Now all eyes cut toward Kurt, like this was a chess match and it was his move.

Kurt turned and walked out, pausing beneath the awning, the rain beating the street with a fury. Alice sidled up next to him, weaving her arm though his, quiet as grass.

"Let's try that Blue Plate Special place down the street," she said.

Kurt couldn't move, his fight or flight response locked into fight mode. About then, the bar clan started singing a raucous song, the words muffled but quite discernible from the sidewalk, the screen door the only thing between Kurt and the choir.

Laughter poured out onto the street, joining the roar of the rain, everyone inside having a grand old time, while Kurt and Alice shivered hungry and cold on the sidewalk. In the distance, beyond the small town, the vast sky rumbled with flashes of lightning.

Disgusted, and discouraged, Kurt directed his anger toward the sidewalk, determined to get some real food at the Blue-Plate Special, even if it meant he had to kill someone for it.

Alice followed, staying close to the store fronts, while Kurt no longer bothered to hide from the rain.

Chapter Sixteen

They had already ordered. Kurt was sitting by himself drinking ice water the waitress had brought over, still stewing over the rude bartender, when Alice returned from the restrooms. She sat opposite Kurt, her attention elsewhere.

"What are you looking at?" Kurt said, noticing that Alice was staring at something across the restaurant.

"That woman looks so familiar," Alice said, unable to pull her eyes away.

Kurt turned in his seat to see the couple entering the restaurant. It was the nosey raven-haired woman from the tavern, and her dashing young man. They took a seat by the front windows.

"That's the woman from the tavern," Kurt said, turning back to his glass of water. "That's why she looks familiar. We saw her ten minutes ago."

Still wearing his white apron, the man came over to Kurt and Alice's table carrying two drinks with ice and set them down. "Here's a couple of Dr Peppers for you both, on the house," the man said.

"We didn't order Dr Peppers," Kurt said.

"I know. I just thought you might enjoy a couple of cold drinks."

"You think we're *scrams*, don't you?"

"Look, nobody pays me to think," the man said. "They pay me to cook and mind my own business, okay. Enjoy your meals." The man started to walk away when Kurt said they didn't want the Dr Peppers.

The man returned to the table. "What's your name?"

"Kurt…and this is my wife, Alice."

"Hi, Alice…So…Kurt, I thought you might enjoy them, because frankly, you seem a bit agitated."

"Did the clown from the tavern call down here?"

As evidenced by the shifting tension in his features, it was obvious the man was working hard to compose himself, trying to avoid a nasty scene. "Kurt, are we gonna have a problem? Because if you can't control yourself, I'm gonna put your food in a bag, and you and Alice are gonna have to eat somewhere else. Okay?"

"Kurt, please…let it drop," Alice said, then shifted her eyes up to the man. "Thank you for the cold drinks."

"You're very welcome," he said. "I'll get your sandwiches right out."

Once the man was back in the kitchen, Kurt sipped the soda the man gave them. "I hate Dr Pepper," he said.

"I know. Just don't drink it, okay."

Kurt noticed Alice staring at the couple again, but before he could say anything, the waitress brought their roast beef sandwiches. Kurt salted his french fries, then squeezed ketchup onto his plate. Before biting into his sandwich, he took a moment to savor the aroma. He couldn't believe how great it smelled, and how much he missed hot food. Alice started eating, stealing glances at the woman across the room. Kurt asked her again why she was so obsessed with her. She said the woman looked familiar, but not because she saw her at the tavern.

"It's deeper than that," Alice said, dipping a French fry into the ketchup.

Kurt and Alice had almost finished with their meal when the waitress came over and asked if they needed anything else. "More Dr Pepper?" she asked Alice, who had downed most of hers.

"No, thank you."

"Sir," the waitress said, addressing Kurt. "You don't care for Dr Pepper? I thought—" The woman cut her sentence, then smiled at Kurt. "I could get you a Coke…"

"No, thanks," Kurt said, wiping his mouth with the napkin, deciding he wasn't going to let anything spoil the wonderful meal he'd just eaten.

"I'll just leave this here," the waitress said, setting the check down near Kurt. "Just bring it to the register when you're ready."

Kurt looked at the bill, then took a deep breath, realizing they had no plan past eating a hot meal. Where would they stay? How would they get back to Rescue? He turned in his chair and took his eyes to the window, the rain a torrent. He was thankful they were not on the road, but he wasn't certain where they could go. Maybe they'd find an inexpensive motel in Ottomon.

He reached toward the back pocket of his coveralls and felt nothing. Buried under all his exuberance and anticipation over finding this town, was the fact that they had no money. That's why he'd broken into all the vending machines. How could he have forgotten so soon!

His stomach clenched, picturing his wallet on the nightstand at home.

"We have a problem, Alice."

"What could possibly—"

"Do you have any money?"

"No…oh my, I totally forgot too…I was so…" she said, her face pulled in worry. She glanced down at their bare, food-stained plates, at her empty glass.

"Okay…okay, I'll handle this," Kurt said.

Kurt cleared his throat, looking around, his eyes meeting the eyes of the dark-haired woman. How far would they make it if they ran? No, they couldn't do that. He'd explain to the proprietor, tell them that he'd send a check as soon as they returned to Rescue. They sat so long, Kurt deciding what to do, that the waitress came over and asked if there was a problem.

"Can I speak to the proprietor?" Kurt asked.

"Was there a problem with the food? The service?"

"No, no, nothing like that."

"Oleg!" the waitress called across the restaurant, drawing the attention of the young couple, and three other diners in blue coveralls at the other end. "Oleg, this couple needs to speak to you."

The man with the apron came out from the kitchen. He looked at Kurt first, then Alice, bringing his eyes back to Kurt. "Yes?"

Kurt stammered, explaining that he'd lost his wallet and that he would send the man a check once they returned to Rescue. "We just have to get back to Rescue, and then I'll send the check right away…"

"Rescue?" The man was shaking his head, smirking. "Don't you work at the Otto plastics plant?"

"No. We work in Rescue."

The man scoffed, his eyes narrowed on Kurt. "I put up with you people because I have to. I try to ignore your outbursts. And your smell. And your stupidity. But I'll be damned if I'm gonna feed you for free!" By now, the man had raised his voice to a decibel that could be heard in the next county over. "I tried to be nice to you, giving you free Dr Pepper, and you pull this shit! No, no more. I've had it!" The man stormed off, headed for the phone behind the counter.

The three scrams at the other table started getting

excited, making noises, until the raven-haired woman went over and calmed them down. She then went to the counter and spoke with the proprietor. The man with the apron became very agitated, shooting glances toward Kurt, until he seemed to give up, throwing his arms in the air, nodding toward the woman, then scratched his head, glancing once more at Kurt before he disappeared into the kitchen.

She came over to Kurt and Alice's table. "Hi, it was just a misunderstanding, but everything is fine now," the woman said.

"I don't understand," Alice said.

"The check's been taken care of…"

"You paid our bill?" Kurt said, growing indignant over this woman's nerve. "You had no right to—"

"I know, but my husband and I wanted to pay for your meal. We saw how they treated you at the tavern, and it was…well, just unwarranted. No one should be treated that way. I hope you'll accept our kindness."

"We don't need your handouts, lady. We have a home and a car…in Rescue. And money in the bank…and… we're not *scrams!*" Kurt cut his eyes toward the people in blue coveralls at the far table, then brought them back.

The woman shook her head, sincerely confused. "I'm sorry, I don't know what those are…*scrams?*"

Kurt knew she was lying; he just didn't know why. She had gone over and spoken to them, even managed to calm them down.

The woman smiled, then was joined by her husband as she walked out the front door.

A volcanic heat rose up in him. He glared over at the scrams, then brought his eyes to Alice, before looking away, shifting to find his tightly-balled fists resting on the table. Suddenly he felt stupid and ashamed, and scared. Without money, they'd be sleeping rough again, like hobos. Indigents. Bums. They'd have no way to pay for train tickets back to Rescue, or a Greyhound bus. When they'd found Ottomon, he figured their troubles were over. Now it seemed they were just starting.

Chapter Seventeen

As they walked from the Blue-Plate Special, Kurt realized they needed different clothes. How was that going to happen without money? The rain had almost stopped, but the sky to the east looked more ominous than it had earlier. A lone car approached slowly from the west, down main street—an older model coral and cream Edsel with broad whitewalls, its dual headlamps glaring off the slick pavement. Kurt had just turned to Alice to suggest they walk back to the rustic rest area when someone spoke.

They both spun around to see the dark-haired woman who had taken care of their bill. She was on the passenger side of the car, with the window rolled down.

"Can we drop you somewhere?" the woman said. "The weather is absolutely dreadful."

Alice froze, falling mute, her eyes as big as quarters. Kurt studied her strange behavior a moment before spinning back to answer the woman. "No, we'll be fine."

"There's a bad storm coming. Do you have a place to stay?"

"We're staying a few miles up the highway. We'll be fine."

The woman opened the passenger-side door, then got out and folded the front seat forward so they could climb in the back. "Please," she said. "It's no problem. Really."

"Well?" Kurt said to Alice.

Alice could only stare at the woman, her face blank.

"Please," the woman said, almost pleading. "We'd be so happy if you'd join us."

Kurt escorted Alice to the car, his hand on her lower back. With both of them situated in the back seat, the young woman got in, closed the door, and they drove toward the highway.

"Hi, I'm Torri," the woman said, extending her hand over the back of the seat toward Alice, then Kurt. "This is my husband, Emmanuel, but everyone calls him Manny." The young man said hello to them from the rearview mirror.

Since Alice had seemed to lose her voice, Kurt figured he had to do the introductions. "This is my wife, Alice, and I'm Kurt."

"Hi Kurt. And Alice, oh, such a lovely name. So where are you both from?"

"Aren't you curious why we're both wearing blue coveralls?" Kurt said, sensing something was very off with these two. "And why we don't have any money?"

The woman stammered, losing her voice temporarily, like Alice. "I...I didn't want to be rude..."

Kurt scoffed. "That didn't seem to be a problem for you at the tavern when you told us we should leave."

"I was just...I don't know. I guess it was rude. I'm sorry. It just seemed things were heating up, and—"

"Want to know what I think?" Kurt said, feeling a new resolve, and tired of the charades. "I think you know what *scrams* are, and I think you knew we weren't *scrams*."

The woman drew a deep breath, taking her attention to her husband, as if surreptitiously asking his advice on what to say next.

"What's going on here?" Kurt said when she didn't answer. He saw the rest area approaching and told Manny to pull in. Manny slowed the car, gravel crunching beneath the tires, and stopped under the single flood light.

"Thanks for the ride," Kurt said, waiting for Manny to get out so he could push the seat forward. Manny didn't move. Kurt pushed on the seat to let Manny know he wanted out. Manny looked over at Torri.

"Please, just wait, okay?" Torri said to Kurt. "We haven't been completely honest. We saw you at the tavern, and yes, we knew you weren't scrams, but we…we just… we knew things weren't going well for you, and just wanted to help. That's the truth of it. We felt bad for you…"

Kurt pushed forward on the back of Manny's seat again, like a rambunctious child too long in the car. "Let us out or there's going to be trouble," Kurt said.

Torri pleaded again. "Please, Kurt, where are you going to stay."

"That's not your concern."

"Well, you and Alice can't stay here at this restroom! It's absolutely dreadful!"

"Where should we go, then?" Alice said softly, rebounding back to life after her self-imposed silence.

Torri swung her eyes toward Alice, her face resplendent with joy and possibilities. "Manny and I found this quaint little hotel just up the road. It's absolutely darling, Alice. With little doilies on the night stands…even on the dressers. They have a quiet bar on the ground floor! It will be so much fun!"

"What about these?" Alice asked, referring to her blue coveralls.

"I know just the thing," Torri said, jumping from the car. "Open the trunk, Manny!"

Torri had opened a suitcase by the time Alice joined her at the rear of the car. Torri pulled out a pink blouse and held it up to Alice. Then grabbed a pair of pleated trousers. "Let's go inside and try these on," Torri said, excited, as if embarking on an impromptu shopping spree. The women disappeared inside the small building, leaving Kurt alone in the backseat, Manny in the front.

"Might as well stretch our legs, Kurt," Manny said, popping open the door and stepping into the parking lot. He withdrew an opened pack of cigarettes from his shirt, then clapped the pack against his palm until a single cigarette shot forward. He held it out to Kurt, which Kurt declined with a wave of his hand. Manny slid it out and wedged it between his lips. He cupped his hands around the end and lit it with his lighter, taking a deep drag and holding the smoke in. The lighter seemed to appear and disappear out of thin air, like a magic trick.

Bursts of lightning flashed in the distance, resembling a string of explosions, the rumbling of thunder low and persistent.

Torri burst from the restrooms, her face a big smile, as she scrambled for personal items from the suitcase, and a few pairs of shoes, then fled back in to join Alice.

Manny meandered to the back of the Edsel, then called Kurt.

Two opened suitcases sat next to one another in the trunk. Manny took another drag on his cigarette, then rummaged through the folded clothes, the cigarette pressed between his lips. He glanced over at Kurt occasionally, sizing him up, before digging his hands back down into the pile.

"You're a big man," Manny said, bending over into the trunk, then squinting as the smoke rolled up into his face. "My jeans and slacks won't fit you, but these should." He came out with a pair of black drawstring cotton sweatpants and handed them to Kurt. Kurt had a few pairs at home that he used for working around the house, and helping Alice in the garden.

Manny shoved a large burgundy sweatshirt into Kurt's hands. "I had one that matched the pants, but I didn't bring it. Go try them on."

Kurt turned to take them into the restroom, actually feeling a bit relieved to get out of the soaked coveralls, and to leave behind the stigma of the scram.

"Wait. Here," Manny said, tossing a pair of gray sport socks toward Kurt. "I know I don't have shoes that will fit you," Manny added, drawing deep on the smoke until the tip glowed like a volcano. A memory rushed back, making Kurt's knees weak; the mechanical man in the driveway who abducted them.

"What's wrong?" Manny said. "The socks? I might have some other socks you—"

"The socks are fine," Kurt said, not sure how to play this. He didn't want to tangle with this fellow unnecessarily. After all, the man was being hospitable, unlike the metal man with the fedora. Manny didn't wear a fedora, as if that fact alone proved Kurt could trust him; what an insane notion.

Kurt padded toward the door with a faded MEN painted on it, unable to find a place to sit and change, he balanced the clothes on the sink and started pulling the wet coveralls off. As he dressed, he thought about Alice, who had rightly been distant, and dubious of the couple, then changed lanes suddenly, basically inviting the woman, Torri, into their lives. It seemed that Alice had warmed to the idea of letting this couple get them a room. He had to admit, after waking up in this smelly bathroom several hours earlier, a bath and bed sounded too good to pass up.

He checked himself in the mirror, then brushed his fingers through his wet hair trying to make something of the tangled mess he was staring at. It seemed pointless, so he smoothed it back from his forehead and down behind his ears. He needed a haircut, that was certain. And a shave! Alice hadn't said anything about his prickly stubble.

"Hey, Kurt, you decent?"

"Yeah, Manny."

Manny came around the corner carrying a toiletries kit. "Here, if you want to grab a shave and brush your teeth. There's an unopened toothbrush, and a Gillette adjustable with…oh, and shaving cream…if you're interested."

"Do you always travel with extra supplies for the destitute?" Kurt was trying to be light, make a joke, but this man's desire to be accommodating seemed unusual.

Manny chuckled. "You're hardly destitute," he said, and left the bathroom, leaving Kurt to rummage through the leatherette bag filled with mouthwash, toothbrushes, toothpaste and shaving gear; a virtual traveling Rexall drugstore. He pulled out the razor, which looked brand new, then opened the blade tray and was pretty sure the blade had never been used, just like the razor. Kurt didn't linger on the puzzle too long, shaking the can before releasing a nice mound of white shaving cream into his palm.

Everyone was back in the automobile when Kurt exited the grungy building. He'd crumpled the coveralls into a ball and stuffed them down into the trash can, his mind replaying hundreds of images from the past several days. Things he was trying to forget. Things he would never forget. Things that could spark retribution; the stolen Oldsmobile, breaking and entering, the vandalized vending machines. And how about the dead man under the fence, his skull smashed to mush. The inventory stole his breath. He just wanted it all to be over, hoping he and Alice would be back in their home in Rescue by this time tomorrow evening.

Chapter Eighteen

Torri fixed her makeup in the bathroom mirror, while Manny flipped through TV channels in their room, checking on the most recent programming. When she finished, she came out and sat on the cushy chair near Manny. "What do you think?" she said.

"About this inane programming?" Manny said. "At the last meeting, Kamdyn, from broadcast and programming told me..." He paused, then faced her and asked, "Do you know Kamdyn?"

"I think I remember him..."

"Anyway," Manny said, reaching for his pack of cigarettes. "Kam tells me they fabricated a hundred seasons of The Adventures of Ozzie & Harriet and almost seventy of Lassie. 'And that's thirty shows per season,' he tells me, grinning like a ghoul. All I could think was, why? No human lived long enough to watch a hundred seasons of anything, much less that silly show."

Torri chuckled, reaching out for the cigarette Manny was offering.

"When I told him as much," Manny said, "he lost his stupid smirk and skulked away."

She smiled, recalling what Zylinda had told her at the last meeting, before Manny had arrived. "We're actually doing some meaningful work in broadcast," Zylinda had whispered to her. "We've fabricated new episodes of *The Twilight Zone*, introducing robots, alternate life forms, non-local intelligence, space travel and space stations. Even computers. Exposing the humans to things they're going to need to be aware of eventually." At the time, Torri wasn't sure any of that was a good idea, especially the computers, but had said nothing.

Torri drew deeply on her cigarette, before releasing the smoke. "Let's talk about the Franklins," she said to Manny.

Manny shut off the television, blowing smoke toward the ceiling. "They're suspicious, especially Kurt." Manny came over and sat on the cushioned foot stool near her chair.

Torri thought about their good fortune, hers and Manny's, finding the Franklins with such ease. But it hadn't all been luck. She and Manny had met after the last meeting, and talked about the Franklins, Manny believing they were in danger. Tori had questioned his assumption, since no one, not even Laudamon who was in charge of the Franklin's sector, seemed to know where they were. Manny had told her about the incident at the Otto plastics plant, that guards had found two dead scrams while shutting down the facility, one in the compound yard near a dead Irish Setter, the dog's head lopped off, the other dead beneath the fencing. Torri couldn't figure out how Manny had made the jump, especially since the Franklins lived in Rescue, which was over 180 miles from the Otto plant. Manny told her that Laudamon believed the Franklins had stolen an Oldsmobile from a resident's home, and took the people's dog with them. At that point, Laudamon had already stopped searching for the them, downgrading their status from Significant to Trivial due to their age.

When she and Manny arrived in Otto earlier that afternoon, they'd spoken to numerous guards from the plastics plant, as well as a few bus drivers, one in particular who told them about a strange middle-aged couple who acted out of character for scrams. "They were dense enough, for sure," the driver had told her. "Maybe too dense. Something was off, though. When I offered them a ride to the barracks, they acted like they weren't interested. Which is totally unlike any scram. They always jump at the chance to get a ride, even if it takes them out of the way. They like riding in motor vehicles."

"How do we take this next step, Manny," she said, puffing on her cigarette. "Do we still go with the virus/inoculation scenario? Do you think they'll go along with it?"

"I don't know, but it's worth a try. You know, if we ask them if they've been inoculated yet, they may get curious and wonder why they'd need to be. Then we can tell them about the virus. And that's that. Mission accomplished." Manny lit a new cigarette and stowed his lighter in his pants pocket.

Torri blew smoke toward the ceiling. "When?"

"Let's see if they want to meet downstairs after they've freshened up. Have dinner and drinks."

"Okay. That makes sense." Torri wondered how much Alice and Kurt knew. They'd already been exposed to scrams, and Kurt would certainly push that subject again. How could they explain them away. And Alice, so lovely. Torri could still remember her little nose when she was two, and her cute little voice.

"Have you heard what we found out about Kensington," Manny said.

"I've been wondering what went wrong."

Manny explained how an investigator had gone to the Franklin's home, then described what she'd found; a damaged bedroom door with a head-sized ragged hole, buckshot pellets lodged in the wallpaper and floor. Torri was having trouble parsing this event. Violence was not part of the collection protocol put forth by the Advisory Parliament and The Illustrious 7. Collection was to be handled with diplomacy and tact, not like a coup or hostile takeover.

Before she could voice her bewilderment over what he'd just shared, Manny brought out an electronic tablet and handed it to her. It appeared Kensington had submitted a memo to the AP outlining a plan he called, "Shock and Reverence; Maintaining Order through Aggression and Fear." She read on, unable to keep from laughing. Kensington's ideas were preposterous, a rambling dissertation on presenting an "indestructible" presence to eliminate any and all ideas around reprisal or returned aggression from humans. It bordered on psychotic.

"Where would Kensington get such a twisted notion?" she asked, chuckling, both confused and amused at the same time. "That's some real Wild West bullshit, there!" Emtrons normally weren't prone to neurosis or psychosis, but some instances had arisen over the centuries. Corrupted circuitry. Maligned algorithms. Anything was possible with machine learning, the intelligence looping back on itself, analyzing itself, negating its own subroutines and programming. Self-perverting. Basically, feeding upon itself…like unborn baby sharks in the womb.

"Wow," she said, shaking her head.

When she reached the part of Kensington's memo addressing the notion of *Conquest through Terror*, she burst out laughing.

"Crazy, right?" Manny said, smiling. He picked up the tablet and got to his feet, telling her he needed to check on some things.

Torri took her cigarette to the hotel room balcony—the

overhanging deck from the room above protecting her from the rain—unable to stop thinking about Alice. Alice was only two when they took her to the new municipal pool that opened in Rescue. Alice, wearing her yellow swimsuit, squealed with laughter and joy when she saw the blue water. She would run up to it and squat down at the edge, splashing water up at Torri with her tiny hand and giggling. When Torri tried to take her into the pool, Alice cried and ran toward Manny who was sitting at a poolside table. Torri came over to pick her up and Alice scooted closer to Manny's leg, wrapping her chubby arms around it. "No, Mommy. No." When Torri went back to sit at the edge of the pool, Alice would rush over laughing, then squat down on the rough concrete on one knee and splash Torri, giggling the whole time. Alice loved the water, just not being in it.

That's when the reality of being an emtron really hit Torri. Watching Alice laugh and cackle with joy at being around the water, splashing in it with her hand, made Torri realize that humans had a capacity for enjoying life, experiencing all the nuance of being alive, that emtrons could never begin to understand merely through words and descriptions and convoluted mathematical algorithms. Torri and Manny were advanced emtrons, supposedly capable of *feeling*—at least something believed to resemble human emotion—through a nearly infinite chain of subroutines consisting of millions of canned responses created to approximate emotion. But seeing Alice react to the water that day at the pool, Torri knew she had never experienced anything close to what her two-year old daughter was capable of feeling; which was both terror and elation, in equal measure, in the span of seconds.

Torri finished her cigarette, flipping it out into the rain, watching it fall two stories to the parking lot below. She tapped another from her pack and lit it, wondering if they should call over to the Franklin's room, find out if they were ready for dinner. Seeing Alice as a grown woman in her fifties, had stirred something in Torri. She wasn't sure she could call it emotion, but it was something.

She puffed a few more times, then flipped the burning cigarette away, no longer interested in it, ready to see if the Franklins wanted to meet for dinner.

After pulling the balcony doors closed behind her, Torri entered the room and saw Manny on his tablet speaking to someone. He glanced in her direction, then ended the transmission.

"I have a *Flit* coming in the morning," he said to Torri.

"In the morning? That's too soon…" Torri said.

"Time's running out, Tori. We have to get them moved."

"I know, but they've had enough shock and awe for a while. Let's see if we can coax them a bit more delicately, okay?"

"Look, Torri, I get it, I do. I asked you to help me because I care about them, about Alice. I was thinking about when she opened her first tricycle that year." Manny chuckled. "I tried to put her on the seat and show her where to put her feet and she screamed bloody murder until I lifted her off…"

"Yeah, all she wanted to do was ring the little bell. I'd forgotten about that." Torri laughed quietly, picturing Alice as if the curly-headed three-year-old was standing in the hotel room with her tricycle, ringing the bell, then looking up at Manny and Alice and giggling.

Torri didn't want to traumatize them anymore if they could avoid it. She was worried the Franklin's would panic upon seeing a foreign craft floating down from the sky like a feather. They had surely seen airplanes, and helicopters, both obnoxiously boisterous and violent. While a *Flit* transport was different from any other aircraft; sleek, with no visible moving parts, and silent as a balloon.

Manny reached across the bedspread for his tablet and tapped the screen a few times with his fingertip. "I cancelled the *Flit*. We'll figure something out."

"Let's call them, Manny, see if they're ready to meet downstairs."

Chapter Nineteen

Alice was still in the bathroom, applying makeup Torri had given her, while Kurt sat on the hotel bed, struggling against the nagging word playing over and over behind his eyes. *Destitute.* Maybe it wasn't the word so much, but more Manny's reaction to it. Kurt had joked with the young man about he and Alice being destitute, and Manny had responded by saying, "You're hardly destitute." Why would the smartly-dressed young man say that, given the facts of their meeting; Kurt and Alice were filthy, and probably smelled horrible, dressed like tramps and had no money to pay for their meal. What could possibly have led Manny to the conclusion that Kurt and Alice were *hardly destitute*? Certainly not the circumstances that Manny and Torri had found them in. Was it just kindness, trying to be sensitive to their impoverished situation, or something more nefarious? Did they in fact know Kurt and Alice were on the run, so to speak, and that they were being hunted? Were Manny and Torri like bounty hunters? Were Kurt and Alice in worse trouble than they thought? The assessment left Kurt with a clawing dread.

When the hotel room phone rang, Kurt stretched across the bed to the nightstand and answered it.

"Yes?"

"This is Manny. Down the hall. You and Alice ready for some dinner and drinks?"

"To be honest, Manny, you both have been too kind already. We can't impose on you anymore. Torri already paid for our lunch today and kept us out of a really bad jam. And then you both get us this fabulous room. Really, it's too much. We hope we can impose on you one last time to give us a ride back to Rescue tomorrow, so we can return this kindness you've shown us," Kurt said, telling Manny everything he and Alice had discussed ahead of time. They were truly grateful, yet more than a little suspicious of their good fortune with the young couple.

"Alice and I want you to spend the night with us in our home in Rescue," Kurt continued. "We have a wonderful spare bedroom. And we'll take you out for a nice dinner. It'll be fun…and I'll feel better having repaid at least a fraction of your generosity."

The phone was silent for too long, Kurt wondering if he had somehow insulted the man, or worse, proposed a burden—driving them back to Rescue—that even for this gracious couple, was a bridge too far. But they needed a ride more than anything, and desperately wanted to return home, get their lives back on track.

"Manny?"

"Oh, sorry. Torri was asking me something and I got distracted. No, no problem driving you back to Rescue tomorrow. We're actually headed that way. It's a slight detour, but not an issue. We love seeing new places…"

"Great! That's really great. So, we'll see you in the morning?"

"Yeah. Say, is Alice around? Torri wanted to ask her something."

"Um…she's indisposed right now. Can I have her phone your room when she's free?"

"Sure, Kurt. Thanks." The man disconnected the call just as Alice walked from the bathroom.

"This is nice, isn't it Kurt?" Alice said.

"What's that?"

"This room. How much do you think it cost?"

"I don't know. But Manny said they'd drive us back to Rescue tomorrow."

Alice didn't respond, which Kurt found odd. She had to be as excited about getting back home as he was. "Oh, Torri wants you to phone her room."

Alice sat on the edge of the bed and dialed their room. Torri picked up on the second ring. "It's Alice."

Kurt could only hear Alice's side of the conversation.

"The makeup was perfect! Thanks so much. I'm not a big makeup person, but I did miss it these past few days." A long pause, Alice fumbling with the phone cord. "Okay, but only on one condition. That you let us repay this extraordinary kindness you've shown us." Another long pause, Alice leaning forward, nodding. "Promise?" Another pause, Alice agreeing silently on some point, smiling this time. "Give us about fifteen minutes. Okay."

Alice reached over and set the phone in the cradle.

"What's going on?" Kurt asked.

"We're meeting them for dinner in fifteen minutes."

Kurt was upset. He and Alice had agreed to spend the evening by themselves, both of them wary of the young couple. "Why did you agree to that?" he said.

"I have something to tell you, and I need you to listen, Kurt. Really listen, okay?"

"I always listen, Alice."

"But this time I need you to *really* listen, because what I'm about to say…you're not going to want to hear…and I need you to hear me…"

Kurt couldn't figure out what this was about. Nothing had happened that Kurt hadn't been present for, unless it was something Torri had said or done in the ladies' room at the rest stop.

"This is going to sound crazy, Kurt, but…Torri is my mother."

Kurt sat back, stunned. "I'm not sure I understand, Alice. Your mother is dead."

"I know, but Torri looks exactly like my mother when I was a young child. She—"

"You can't go on that! You were young, and…it was decades ago. How can you possibly think—"

"I know, Kurt. I told myself the same thing. But it's not just her appearance. It's something more, her expressions and mannerisms, nuances that imprint on children over time, unexplainable details that—"

"That's crazy, Alice. She's probably half your age."

"Remember the photo on the fridge at Bella's house?"

Kurt didn't know a Bella, or recall any photo on a refrigerator. When would this have happened?

"Bella…the Irish setter that…" Alice's expression turned gloomy. She closed her eyes a moment to reset. "The house where we stole the Oldsmobile. Where you sewed up my wound." Alice pulled her blouse up to show him the red area of the wound, the floss he'd found.

"I don't recall a photo—"

"The one I showed you on the freezer door. The woman and her husband standing with two children. I told you she was my mother."

"I think you said she *looked* like you mother. I don't remember you saying—"

"Yes, you do. You even questioned me on it…"

The photo on the freezer door came back blurry in his mind. There was a dark-haired woman in the photo, and her husband, presumably, standing behind two children, all smiling, but he could never concede for sure that the woman was Torri, or even looked like her. How could Alice be so sure? Kurt tried to picture his own parents, bringing forth vague likenesses—yes, that was them, but were these merely impressions that matched his projections? He certainly couldn't draw them from memory, but then, he couldn't draw. Could he describe them to a sketch artist? Probably not with any accuracy.

Kurt thought back to the Blue-Plate Special diner, how Alice had turned suddenly aloof and distant for no real reason, but he couldn't recall what had precipitated the odd behavior. Was that when Alice thought she recognized this Torri woman? What had happened? Alice had said the young lady looked familiar. But that's not unusual, to see someone who *reminds* you of someone else. Yet that wasn't what Alice was saying now, that Torri *reminded* her of her mother. She was saying Torri *was* her mother.

"Help me understand why you are so sure?" Kurt said.

"Remember when we walked out of the Blue-Plate Special restaurant," Alice said, "and Torri and Manny drove up to offer us a ride? It was pouring rain, and you told her we were fine. Torri asked if they could drop us somewhere, then added, 'The weather is absolutely dreadful.'"

Kurt still didn't get it, nor did he recollect that exact exchange, but it apparently meant something to Alice. Kurt shrugged.

"My mother said that to me all the time. When I'd come home from school and told her that some girl picked on me, she'd say, 'Oh, Alice, that's absolutely dreadful.' Anything that happened that was bad, she'd say, 'that's absolutely dreadful.' Then at the rest area, she said it again, remarking that we couldn't stay at that place because it was, 'Absolutely dreadful!'"

Kurt conceded that it was not a very common turn of phrase, but hardly proof of something so outlandish as what Alice was claiming.

"Who talks like that, Kurt? My friends' parents never said things like that. Our friends don't talk that way. I don't know of anyone who does. It's kind of hoity-toity, you know? Pretentious, affected, but we weren't wealthy, as you know. Maybe her parents were, but I never met my grandparents. If they were rich, we never received any of their money."

They stared at each other, Kurt wanting to feel this connection as deeply as Alice did. What would that mean if Torri actually was Alice's mother? Something too profoundly terrifying to imagine, as if the last few days hadn't been disturbing enough.

"Why are you telling me this?" Kurt finally said, wishing it hadn't sounded as harsh as it had.

Alice took her gaze to the floor, then brought her eyes to Kurt. "I want to know more about her. About them. I think...I think maybe they have something to do with what's been happening to us, or at least know something about it. That's why I agreed to dinner tonight."

Something was bothering Kurt. "Is Manny your father, then?"

Alice screwed up her face, pondering on it. "I don't recognize him at all, to tell the truth..."

Kurt exhaled, nodding. "Fair enough. Let's get some answers." He knew an explanation must exist, but it certainly wasn't going to be that Torri, a woman in her thirties, was Alice's mother! That was too absurd for him to even consider, yet he could see no harm in going along with Alice's conviction, no matter how nutty it sounded.

Alice grabbed the sweater Torri had given her, and waited for Kurt to put on his cruddy shoes.

"Alice?"

"Yes, Kurt?"

"What are we going to do if they ask how we got in this mess?" Just then, another notion hit him before she could answer. "Or worse, what are we going to do if they don't ask?"

"I don't understand," Alice said.

Kurt hesitated, trying to untangle the logic behind his own statement, which, just moments earlier, made perfect sense. Now his mind was a cloud. "I'm not sure I do either. Let's just eat."

Chapter Twenty

Torri waved from the table when Kurt and Alice entered the bar. Manny stood up to shake Kurt's hand while Torri hurried over to hug Alice, remarking on how nice she looked. Already it was weird. Like they were all old friends, or family, sharing a connection with no basis or substance in reality. To make it even stranger, Kurt was unable to detach from Alice's extraordinary claim about Torri being her *mother*. He loved Alice, and for as long as he'd known her, she had never been given to fanciful thinking, or outrageous assertions. She'd always been pragmatic, realistic; now, he didn't know what to think.

"Let's order, then we can talk," Torri said, pushing menus toward everyone.

The bartender came and took the orders, then brought drinks. Torri instructed him to put it on their room.

"So, you're from Rescue," Torri said, steepling her hands in front of her, her elbows resting on the table. "That's a long way from Ottomon." She waited, smiling, as if that should be enough for them to start sharing their peculiar adventure. Kurt glanced at Alice, then back to Torri, trying to see a resemblance. He couldn't find one.

The silence was becoming awkward, until Torri tried another tact. "Were you vacationing and...something went wrong?"

"If you consider being abducted by an insane robot wearing a fedora, *vacationing*, then yes, a lot went wrong on our vacation," Kurt said, not bothering to conceal his frustration with where things were already heading.

Torri's expression turned dark, shocked even, if Kurt was reading her right. Manny grimaced, folding his hands in his lap.

"Abducted? Robots? I don't think I understand," Torri said.

"See, that's the funny part," Kurt said. "I actually think you *do* understand...both of you do." Kurt shifted his eyes between the two of them. Manny let his eyes drop, and Torri appeared hurt by the accusation.

"What Kurt means," Alice started to say, "is that some strange things have been happening to us since this intruder came and took us from our home." She paused. "Not the least of them being...meeting the two of you. Don't get me wrong, we appreciate everything you've done, but it's curious that you showed up in our lives when you did, and...and..."

"And?" Torri said.

"And that you, Torri, bear such a striking resemblance to my own mother, Margaret," Alice said.

"Who's very dead," Kurt added. "For a long time!"

Torri stood up. "Please excuse me just a moment," she said, leaving the table for the restrooms.

"She's fine," Manny said. "And I'm sorry you find it strange, and it makes sense. Total strangers helping total strangers and all. But we are glad to help. Really. And I'm sorry to hear about the abduction. That is disturbing.... Have you spoken with the authorities?"

"Haven't had a chance," Kurt said.

"How did you escape?" Manny asked. "Or did the kidnapper just let you go?"

"No, I don't think he had intentions of letting us go," Kurt said. "We escaped during a car crash that ended up killing the man. And we've been running ever since. We even had a silent air craft tracking us in the woods, but they gave up after two nights." Kurt inhaled deeply, the images of the bizarre events playing through his mind like a movie at three times normal speed. He took a long pull from his glass of Budweiser, thinking how inane this conversation was becoming, everyone pretending this was some kind of normal story. Kurt wanted to scream, but instead, tipped back his Budweiser and finished it.

Torri approached the table and sat down, her pleasant demeanor from earlier gone. Before any meaningful dialogue could resume, not that there would be any, the bartender started setting down food, going back to retrieve the last couple of entrees.

"Does anyone need anything else?" the bartender asked. "Another Budweiser for you sir?"

Kurt shook his head no.

A heavy silence fell over the table, everyone picking at their food, no one seeming hungry anymore.

"Are you my mother?" Alice said into the void, addressing Torri.

"How could you ask such an absolutely dreadful question like that?" Torri said, glaring at Alice.

Alice scoffed and looked over at Kurt, then took a bite of her mashed potatoes. When she finished chewing, she wiped her mouth and said, "We broke into a house so Kurt could attend my wound from the accident." She pulled up the bottom edge of her blouse so they could see. "He sewed it up with dental floss he found—"

"Have you had that looked at by a doctor?" Torri asked, genuinely concerned. "It looks a bit red."

"We really haven't had a chance to find a doctor…" Alice said, then continued her story. "You see, we didn't even know these people. We just helped ourselves to their stuff. Drank their coffee. Ate their toast and jam. We even ended up stealing their dog and car." Alice chuckled. Even Kurt found it funny, the idea of stealing someone's car, and their dog. "But the strangest part," Alice said, "was, that on their freezer door was a photo of you with two children I've never seen before, as if you were their mother, too. How is that possible, Torri?"

At this, Manny stared over at Torri. Torri was shaking her head, then looked up at Kurt, then Alice, and said, "If you think the past few days of your life have been strange, I'm afraid you won't be prepared at all for what's coming…"

Kurt was taken aback by her statement, never expecting her response to be so candid. When he managed to gather himself, he said, "Does any of this have to do with Leviathan?" Kurt asked, recalling what the guard had said in the Otto plant.

Alice turned toward him with surprise. "You never said anything about *Leviathan*."

"Because I don't know what it is…but I think we're about to find out." Kurt hadn't told her because he'd forgotten all about it, until this moment. The word had spontaneously spilled forth like an omen.

"Leviathan has everything to do with what's happening," Torri said. "If not for Leviathan, we wouldn't be here with you, and you both would still be in Rescue living your lives, never having been abducted."

Kurt waited, reaching over beneath the table to find Alice's hand. She squeezed his hand tightly, her skin warm against his. He couldn't recall the last time he'd held her hand like this. He gazed at Torri, whose expression had gone blank. With all the young woman's generosity, and her affable nature, Torri still came off, at least to Kurt, as someone who could not be trusted, as if she dispensed truth in miserly amounts, and only if, and when, it served her purpose.

"Leviathan," Torri stated, demonstrating great restraint, as if the disclosure required careful deliberation, "is a deadly virus spreading across the country with ferocious speed."

Kurt listened to her explain about three-part inoculations, and controlled environments, watching her lips the way someone might study a ventriloquist, waiting for the slightest clue to the deception. In Kurt's case, he was sure she was lying, but couldn't figure how he knew. Was it from her facial expressions, though she showed little emotion. Maybe that was it, the lack of emotion. But she certainly projected concern, and a gravity around the situation that was warranted. If it was even true.

Just then he recalled something he'd overheard from the guard at the Otto plant, something about the *chance* of Leviathan *hitting*. Neither of those words fit with what Torri was telling them. There was either a virus, or there wasn't. It had hit, or it hadn't. There was no percentage or chance involved, unless the guard had been referring to the mortality rate for those catching the virus. But the guard had been very cavalier about the existence of Leviathan, as if he didn't believe it was going to be a viable threat. Nothing was lining up between what Kurt had overheard, and what Torri was relating.

"Let me stop you, Torri," Kurt said. "We're not going with you to some specialized lab to be inoculated, because the truth is…there's nothing to inoculate against…is there?"

"Kurt! This is serious," Alice said, letting go of his hand under the table. "Remember what Sally was saying about the virus…And the news bulletin by Walter—"

"Yes, I do, Alice," Kurt said, trying to reassure her. "I also remember Sally telling us about people who had recently gone missing. Like we would have, if I hadn't wrestled that crazy robot off the damn highway!"

Alice fell quiet, taking her eyes to Torri, as if waiting for clarification.

"This is nonsense!" Kurt shouted, drawing looks from other patrons in the bar. "I don't know why she's lying, Alice, but she is. I'm sorry, Torri, but for some reason, you just can't be straight with us."

Kurt stood, looking at Alice, imploring her with his eyes to come with him. "Let's go back to our room."

"But, Kurt, we need to—"

"He's right, Alice," Torri said. "I am lying to you."

Chapter Twenty-One

Torri and Manny remained in the hotel bar after Kurt and Alice left the dining area to head back to their room. The bartender came over. "Was there a problem?" he asked, looking down at Kurt and Alice's unfinished meals.

"No, no problem," Torri said. "When are you leaving?"

"As soon as you all check out. We're headed for the D-9 station; I think."

"That's one of the new ones," Manny said. "Very nice. You'll like it."

"Maybe, but I have to say, I prefer being down here."

Torri nodded. "Yes, it's special, to be sure. Thanks for putting this all together on such short notice," Torri added.

"Glad to do it," the bartender said. "We hadn't completely shut down yet, so it was easy. And fun, actually. I'm gonna miss it. Anyway, take your time. No rush."

Torri smiled at him before he walked away, then looked over at Manny, shaking her head. "How could Alice recognize me and not you?" she finally said to him.

"I had my appearance altered after I left P&N, don't you remember? For a university teaching position. I'd been working construction when We were raising Alice, and the board wanted me to look more refined, not so big and gruff…"

She hadn't remembered, but now she did, sort of. It was so long ago. Plus, she never kept up with Manny once their term with Alice was over. It had lasted about ten years. That's when they were reassigned to another newborn. After ten years, the Procreation & Nurture Council brought in new surrogate parents for Alice, Torri and Manny lookalikes, though aged slightly, nothing a ten-year-old would ever notice when she came home from school one day. The new surrogates would take Alice through the next fifteen years, or until she got married and moved out. New, older lookalikes, would then be installed. Since they wouldn't be seen on a daily basis, the changes would not be jarring. Those surrogates could then be aged as needed. The P&N had many scenarios for making seamless switches, eliminating any issues that could raise suspicion for the children about their parents.

"What are we going to do, Manny? This has gone so wrong. They'll never trust us now."

"Well, we can drive them back to Rescue and…let them get on with their life."

She scowled. "Seriously? Just let them be killed?"

"We don't know for sure that will be the outcome…I mean, in some ways, maybe it's more humane…you know, die now or die later."

She scoffed. "I don't get you at all. You were the one who convinced me to come with you, to find them. What's the point if we don't try to salvage them?"

"*Salvage* them?"

"You know what I meant! *Save!*" She turned away, pointing her eyes straight ahead. "We have to think of something. They already know that weird things are going on. It will haunt them the—"

"What do they really know, Torri? They met some

scrams. So, what? They would eventually forget about them, and—"

"You're forgetting about Kensington! They know he wasn't human, that he was some kind of *robot*. Wasn't that what Kurt called him? I mean, Kensington was hardly a *robot*. But to them, Jeez, he was, *not of this world*…how could they ever put that behind them?"

"Humans are resilient. In time, the encounter might become nothing but a strange recollection, maybe even fade enough for them to question the validity of their memory, wondering if it happened at all. They have no proof."

"There has to be a better solution than hoping they just forget…"

"Are you suggesting The Horizon Protocol?"

She spun around to face him. "That's mostly theoretical, Manny. That could screw them up worse than they already are. Horizon's never been tested, as far as I know? Has it? Do you know something about that?"

"No, not really…. It's never been tested with actual humans. But they've run countless trials and simulations—"

"Then we have no idea what effect it will have on humans."

Manny sat back and finished his beer.

"Is that stuff any good?" Torri asked, pointing at his empty beer glass.

"I don't know. *Good* is such a relative term. The beer goes in, the beer comes out. Not sure I would call it *good*. Humans seem to love it. You should just try one some time."

Torri lit up a cigarette and took a deep draw, releasing the smoke slowly. "Do you think they'll leave, Manny?" Torri asked with a bit of urgency.

"Where would they go?" Then, after a moment's thought. "I guess they could if they were too freaked out."

"We need a plan, Manny. Maybe we should just tell them about Leviathan," Tori said, wondering why she hadn't just told them when Kurt brought it up. That was the moment they would've been receptive, but she'd floundered, caught up in her own deliberations. Now, telling them about Leviathan, would seem like some elaborate lie she'd concocted to bend them to her will. It could work, though, maybe give them a sense of urgency, make them willing to set aside their distrust long enough for her to get them to safety.

Torri looked up when the bartender hurried over.

"Your friends are leaving," he said, pointing. "They just walked out."

Chapter Twenty-Two

Kurt didn't want to hear it. As far as he was concerned, they were better off hitchhiking out on the highway than with this couple—no matter how nice they seemed—who wouldn't know the truth if it ran them over. Alice protested—was still protesting as they stood on the shoulder of the dark, wet highway, Kurt with his thumb out—that they should stay, find out what the couple knew. According to Alice, based on her recognition of Torri, the couple knew a lot, and even if they weren't willing to tell her and Kurt, the couple had agreed to give them a ride back to Rescue.

"Plus, we could at least get a good night's sleep, instead of standing in the freezing drizzle trying to beg a ride on a deserted highway!" Alice was clearly more upset than Kurt had ever seen her.

"You don't know if they really planned to drive us home, Alice." Kurt couldn't explain why he was so upset, not without hurting Alice's feelings. The truth was, he never believed for a second that Torri was her mother, the woman who raised her. It was insane. How could he tell her she was insane? Or that her belief was certifiable. He couldn't understand what Alice had seen, or *heard*, from the young woman that had planted this ridiculous notion. A turn of phrase proved nothing. And Alice's assertion that this stranger looked exactly like her mother. Delusional was the word that came to mind. Even so, Kurt couldn't bring himself to pin that characterization on his beloved wife and friend. It was confounding to say the least.

Kurt pulled the hood up on the sweatshirt Manny had given him, glancing over at Alice, her hair stringy and soaked, dripping down her back. Kurt pulled his sweatshirt off and handed it to her. "Put this on before you catch pneumonia."

"Let's go back, Kurt. Please." Alice made no move to take the sweatshirt from Kurt.

"Please put this on," he pleaded, pushing it toward her.

She spun away and started walking back in the direction of the hotel.

"Alice! Wait! Come on, Alice, don't do this."

He jogged after her, the highway as dark as the inside of a black sock. When he caught up to her, he spun her around, asking her to put the hooded sweatshirt on and he'd go back with her. She said nothing, took the garment and dragged it down over her head, then pulled the hood up and resumed her trek toward the hotel.

Kurt fell in behind her, the cold drilling down into his skin. The hotel was no more than a fifteen-minute walk, but it had turned frigid, the rain beating white sparks along the black pavement. Blinding headlights approached, the reflections in the wet surface making them appear like fiery torches. The car slowed to a stop, the window coming down. "Please, Alice, Kurt, get in. It's absolutely dreadful out here!"

Alice glared at Torri, then cut a hard look back at Kurt, as if she knew that Kurt didn't believe her, maybe even thought she was crazy. "Thanks, but no thanks," Alice told

Torri, walking past the car. "I just want to go back to the hotel, stand under a hot shower, and go to sleep."

"Alice, you're soaked. Please get in," Torri said, opening the door. Manny was backing up slowly to match Alice's pace.

"Look lady," Kurt said, "she wants to walk back to the hotel, so, just leave her alone."

"Kurt. Come on," Torri said. "This is nuts. Please, the both of you, just get in and we'll drive you back. Then you can go do whatever you want."

Kurt plodded behind Alice, water dripping from his hair, down his back, his leather shoes waterlogged from the deep puddles. He could feel his socks squishing with each step.

Torri got out and caught up to Kurt, then continued on to Alice. "Come on, Bean. Let us give you a ride…"

Alice spun around to face Torri. "What did you call me?" Alice said, clearly upset.

CHAPTER TWENTY-THREE

Torri brought a dry change of clothes to their room. They agreed to meet in Torri's room when Kurt and Alice were ready. Kurt had been content to put on the dry clothes and fresh socks, eschewing a shower until later, while Alice said she needed some time under the hot water, not only to warm up, but to process the fact that Torri knew a name that only her mother had ever called her; *Bean.*

Kurt was thrown by Alice's disclosure; how could this perfect stranger possibly know Alice's pet name. He didn't even know it. Alice had never mentioned it to him, ever.

Sitting on the edge of the bed, he dried his hair with an extra towel, waiting for Alice to finish up. When she emerged, she had a white towel wrapping her chest and torso. "I'll only be a minute," she told Kurt, then went back into the bathroom carrying her clothes and the makeup bag Torri had given her, then closed the door.

If Kurt allowed himself, he could almost believe every-thing was as it had always been. Alice never liked to dress in front of him. That bit of normalcy brought him a moment's peace, as if they were only a day away from getting their unremarkable life back. Yet some deeper dread was always present, a vine of foreboding creeping and crawling up from his gut.

When Alice emerged the next time, she was dressed and had applied a spare amount of makeup. Years ago, she had told him that applying a smudge of lipstick and a bit of eyeliner lifted her spirits. He could only understand it in terms of shaving, which he did every morning, no matter what, until the past several days while they were fleeing the unknown. Hopefully, that *unknown* would be revealed very soon.

Standing in front of the mirror above the sink, Alice brushed her hair. A moment later she announced she was ready to go.

Kurt got to his feet, aware that Alice had been very quiet on the ride back to the hotel with Torri and Manny. That didn't change when they got back in their room; Alice said nothing, as if she were budgeting words and didn't want to waste any. She had just gone into the bathroom and started the shower.

When they reached Torri and Manny's room, Alice rapped gently on the door. Torri greeted them. "I'm glad my clothes fit you so well, Alice," she said, ushering them over to the floral-print divan. Kurt and Alice sat down, Kurt wondering where Manny was. Alice sat in the chair opposite them.

"Where's your husband?" Kurt asked.

"He's down at the bar—No wait," Torri said, interrupting herself. "First off, Manny is not my husband, okay. No more lying. He is down at the bar, but only because I wanted to talk with the both of you alone. Manny and I just work together occasionally."

Kurt was thankful for that bit of honesty, putting him more at ease.

"I will answer as many questions as I can…but let me start off by telling you about Leviathan. I wasn't lying when I told you before that if not for Leviathan, we would never have met, and you both would still be in Rescue living your lives."

Torri paused as if to take a deep breath—though Kurt couldn't be sure she actually had— then continued, but not before leaning back in her chair. "Leviathan is an enormous asteroid," she said, pausing just a moment. "And it's headed for Earth."

"You mean one of those rocks in outer space?" Kurt said, remembering a program he'd watched a month or two ago, then recalled the bright spot in the daytime sky he and Alice had seen a few days ago. Was it possible they could actually see it?

"Yes. Many of them are relatively small, some only the size of dust particles…. However, Leviathan…Leviathan is four to five miles across, massive enough to extinguish all life on the planet."

Alice's hand shot up to her mouth. Torri wasn't lying this time; that Kurt was certain of. An uncomfortable void opened in his chest. What she had just told them squared with what the guards had discussed at the plastics plant, the one guard feeling confident Leviathan would never *hit*.

Never hit.

That had meant nothing at the time.

The guard had mentioned something about a *forty-seven percent chance* of it happening.

Another very troubling snatch of that conversation bubbled up; "*In two weeks, it may not even be here!*"

The guard had been referring to the expansive Otto Plastics Plant. At the time, Kurt had tried to figure out how the factory could possibly be gone in two weeks. Where would it go? He wondered if they were tearing it down. Now he knew.

Two weeks.

That was a day or so ago.

Twelve days. Maybe less. Was that all the time they had left?

Alice was first to speak. "Is there any way to stop it?"

"No, Alice. Believe me, we've been working on the problem for months."

"So…what can we do?"

"That's why Kensington, the man who abducted you, came to your house. He was tasked with getting you both to safety. But he went about it all wrong. He didn't follow the Noah guidelines. And I'm sorry for that."

"Noah?" Kurt said, curious about the moniker and what it inferred.

"It's just the name we gave to the retrieval project. We're trying to get the inhabitants of Earth to safety."

"Where on Earth," Kurt said, "no pun intended, would it be safe if this asteroid is capable of ending all life on the planet?"

Torri smiled, not a friendly facial expression, but a troubled one. "Would you submit to a procedure to put you both to sleep? Like an anesthetic? You wouldn't be harmed in any way, I promise…" Torri shifted her eyes between the two of them, as if trying to size up their comfort levels. Kurt's drawn face left no doubt as to how he felt about it.

"Why?" Kurt said. "Why is knocking us out necessary? What are you hiding?"

Torri looked at the floor, as if searching for the right answer. "There are things that could cause you great consternation if you knew…knowledge that could make your lives difficult moving forward. Things that might cause you to doubt the very world you're living in…It could cause serious mental issues…"

To Kurt's ears, this was sounding worse and worse. *Scrams!* Is that how they ended up like that; violent, idiotic and dull? Had they *learned* things that destroyed their minds? "Like the scrams?" Kurt said, sitting forward. "Is this knowledge you're speaking of the reason for *their* mental problems?"

Torri seemed thrown by the question for a moment before she recovered. "No, no...not at all. The scrams... that phenomenon is something altogether different. A totally different conversation."

"What if we don't want to be put to sleep?" Alice said. "Are other people agreeing to be anesthetized?"

Yes, Kurt thought. Great question, Alice! What about the rest of the people on Earth? Were they being put to sleep? And taken where? An underground bunker, maybe? He'd seen those on television, underground shelters to protect against nuclear wars. Or are people being whisked away to the center of a mountain, like the NORAD facility in Colorado? Was that safe from a planet-destroying asteroid? How many people could fit in that? And food for that many people? The questions had become too mind-boggling to consider.

"Many people have already gone into a deep sleep and been moved to a very secure and safe location. Sleeping comfortably...unaware they're even there. Unaware of the asteroid and potential danger. If the asteroid misses Earth, and there is a very good chance it could, those sleeping masses will go back to their lives none-the-wiser of the catastrophic events they avoided."

"Where are they?" Kurt said, wanting answers to the questions bouncing around in his mind.

"I prefer to not tell you, as that is knowledge that will send us down the rabbit hole, so to speak, and could cause you both great psychological damage." Torri held Kurt's gaze. "You already know more than those people ever will, and that too is another conversation depending on your decision."

"How long do we have to decide?" Alice asked.

"Unfortunately, not long. Kensington's botched retrieval has cost us all precious time. I hope you can decide by tomorrow morning at the latest. That's why it was so important for you to come back here with us tonight."

"Why didn't Manny want to be a part of this discussion?" Kurt blurted out, exasperated with the direction of things. Too many unknowns. "Why haven't you told us who you work for? How is it possible you are Alice's mother? You should be dead! How is it Kensington looked human and acted human, but wasn't? Was he a robot? Or some kind of alien life form? I've seen that kind of thing on *Star Trek!*" Kurt took a breath, shocked he was now equating reality with a TV show. "And what happened to the scrams to make them that way? And who are you? Are you and Manny both robots like Kensington?" Kurt took a deep breath. "How could we possibly agree to your proposal without having the complete picture?"

"To answer your first question, Manny and I wanted to speak with one voice, and Manny agreed it was best for him to sit this one out." Torri went quiet for a moment, then: "I know this doesn't seem fair, keeping you in the dark, but it really is for your own well-being. I cannot stress enough the danger of answering all these other questions. There is no taking back the answers, and they will haunt you for the rest of your life. That's why we had hoped to spare humanity the discomfort of knowing, by letting them sleep through this tumultuous chapter in human history. That's really all I can say. Anything past what I've already told you will mark the point of no return for you and Alice."

Kurt believed everything she said, that it truly was to his and Alice's advantage to enter blindly into this agreement. Nevertheless, Kurt could never forget what he'd already seen, already knew about scrams, and especially about Kensington. He tried to imagine what he and Alice's life would be like right now if this Kensington robot guy had followed the protocols set out by—who-knows-who?

—another question Kurt would most likely never have an answer to. Could he live with all these questions on the other side of this calamity? And what would happen to them, in deep sleep in this so-called secure location, wherever it was, if the asteroid did in fact strike Earth, destroying everything? Would they—all the inhabitants of the planet—be kept in a deep sleep? And for how long? Or would they be awakened to the disaster Torri and her bunch had tried to protect them from? Then what? Would the retrieval of people, this Noah Project, have been nothing more than a futile attempt to prolong the inevitable? What was the point? Kurt felt his mind collapsing under the weight of the unknowns.

CHAPTER TWENTY-FOUR

After telling Torri they needed time to discuss their options, Kurt and Alice walked back to the room. Alice was quiet, while Kurt talked about all the questions wheeling through his mind. New ones leaped forward as he related the most pressing ones, the ones that confounded him most.

"What about you, Alice? What questions do you have?"

She closed her eyes, sipping from the glass of water she'd gotten from the bathroom faucet. "I am remembering all the moments of my childhood with my mother, unable to figure out how Torri could have been my mother, Margaret, and how she can be the same age as she was when she was raising me? That's the question I need the answer to the most." She hesitated, obviously mulling over the same inconceivable facts Kurt was wrestling with.

"I don't know what our options are if we choose to remain awake?" Kurt said. "Besides, I don't know why we can't just be moved to the safe location right now. What's so secret that they are unwilling to risk exposure. And what difference would it make, anyway, especially if everyone else is asleep?"

"I don't think it's about what they don't want us to know, as much as it is about us not being able to deal with what they tell us. I think they are trying to protect us, not only from the asteroid, but from the knowledge they are convinced will destroy us."

Kurt scoffed. "What could possibly be so alarming? I don't get it."

Alice took a deep breath, letting it out slowly. "I guess the question is, do we want to be given a truth that could ruin our lives regardless of what happens to Earth, or do we want to fall asleep and be spared the horror Torri is convinced will destroy any chance at a normal life?"

Kurt shook his head, knowing that if they didn't get answers now, they never would. How important were the answers? Kurt tried to imagine his new life with Alice. Back in Rescue, the asteroid safely on its path away from Earth, them living with the memory of scrams, and lunatics. As hard as he tried, he could not imagine living with this knowledge. No matter how much Torri was trying to protect them from further mind-wrecking facts! Just the things he'd already been exposed to had altered his life irreparably. A television show depicting robots would no longer be fiction. There would always be the risk of coming across scrams. And Torri, a woman who was supposedly dead for years was in fact still alive, and ageless. How could anyone live a normal life with those realities in your head? The memories would never fade, never wither and die. Nothing would ever be the same. How much worse could it be to know the truth, especially if the *truth* could make sense of scrams and robots? Kurt shook his head, astounded by the thoughts replaying in his mind—*if the truth could make sense of scrams and robots*—as if his mind had already conceded to the notion of these curious anomalies. And why shouldn't his mind acquiesce?—robots and scrams were now part of his new paradigm. Time, no matter how much he had left, would never erase that.

"We need to know, Alice," he said, nearly frantic that he had almost assented to following blindly, to being put to sleep, spared some awful truth. How bad could it be? "We need to know everything."

Alice got up, went to the balcony doors and stepped outside. Kurt sighed, his resolve growing one second, dying the next, his mind on tilt. He was starting to doubt he could handle any truths beyond the ones he was already losing the battle to. *Scrams! Robots! World-ending asteroids!*

Sleep would come as a great comfort, whether he ever woke up or not.

The thought of someone looking over them, protecting them from disaster, left him with a warm feeling of calm.

Losing the battle with his thoughts, Kurt went out to join Alice on the balcony. Rain splashed along the street below, dark puddles dancing in the parabolas of light from the street lamps. Alice was leaning forward, like the figure-head on the prow of a ship, her white fingers wrapping the handrail, the front of her blouse becoming damp from the angle of the rain. He stood next to her—raindrops hitting his face—seized by a surprising peace in the simplicity of this moment. If they could finish out their lives right here, right now, suspended between *knowledge* and *ignorance*, allowing the rain to nurture them, and comfort them with uncomplicated clarity, then there was nothing to decide, nothing to run toward, or away from.

Alice turned to Kurt. "I love you," she said.

She kissed him on the lips, then drew back and went inside. He followed in silence, knowing they had made their decision without ever speaking a word.

CHAPTER TWENTY-FIVE

They didn't wait until morning to tell Torri. The attractive young woman was still dressed when she let them into the room, as if she hadn't bothered going to sleep. Manny was still gone, though Kurt figured the hotel bar had closed hours ago. It was after two in the morning.

"So, you've decided, then?" Torri said.

Alice nodded. "We want to know everything."

Torri's expression wilted under the news. She swung her eyes toward Kurt, then back to Alice. "You're both sure about this?"

"Absolutely sure," Alice said. Kurt took Alice's hand in his, as if to add to her resolve, or bolster his own.

"Okay…" Torri said, the moment playing out with an awkwardness Kurt had not anticipated. They all stood motionless, like stuck wheels, waiting for one or the other to pull them out of the mud. Torri was the first to speak. "I have to make some arrangements…then I'll come to your room. We can start tonight, or wait until morning, after you've had some sleep."

"I doubt either of us will sleep," Kurt said.

Torri sighed, almost inaudibly, though Kurt had picked up on something.

"I guess we should go back and wait, Kurt," Alice said, turning away to smile over at Torri. Alice's smile faded as she grabbed the knob, pulling the door open. Kurt followed her into the hallway. They made their way quietly along the gray and green woven carpeting to the room. Once inside, Alice busied herself packing up the few things Torri had given her—makeup, extra clothes, the hair brush.

"This is the right choice, isn't it Alice?"

Alice turned from the mirror. "I think it's the only choice, Kurt...not even a choice, really."

Chapter Twenty-Six

Torri drove, with Alice seated beside her in the front passenger side. Kurt sat in back, directly behind Alice. Torri explained that Manny had left earlier that evening, that he had things to attend to. Kurt wondered where he could have gone without the car, but didn't bother asking. There were already too many mysteries, too many riddles, and so much dread Kurt could barely breathe. Alice, on the other hand, appeared to be gliding effortlessly through the maelstrom of imponderables.

Kurt's attention shifted between the Edsel's headlights burning a path down the dark highway, and the back of Alice's head, the fragrance of her shampoo wafting toward him now and again.

The rumble of tires on pavement mixed, with the roar of air rushing past the closed windows, filled the vehicle. With the radio off, compressed into the void of conversation, the interior was beginning to feel like a sealed tomb. Torri didn't bother telling them where they were headed, and they didn't ask, both of them convinced all would be made clear very soon.

They had driven about an hour, Kurt figured, when Torri slowed and made a right turn into a paved vacant lot, coming to a stop. As far as Kurt could tell, they were in the middle of nowhere, which sent a shiver of fear though him. Was Torri going to kill them? That idea had never crossed his mind until now.

Torri switched off the engine, then turned off the lights; the world suddenly solid black, formless. Kurt was about to speak but felt uneasy making any noise at all. They sat perfectly still, staring out the windshield without uttering a word. How long would this go on? Kurt checked the side window briefly, then gazed toward Torri, who hadn't moved a muscle as far as he could tell. Alice too was like a statue. Was this part of The Horizon Protocol, sitting in this dark parking lot waiting? Waiting for what? Torri had mentioned the Horizon thing as she was escorting them down to the car earlier. The name was ominous enough. The mystery around it, nearly unbearable. Now this.

Seconds later, lights descended from the sky, completely silent, and came to rest fifty feet from the Edsel. Torri got out and motioned for Kurt and Alice to follow her. Alice got out and waited for Kurt, taking his hand as they walked across the lot. A door on the aircraft opened, unfolding to become a ramp, that settled onto the pavement. Blue lights beneath the craft illuminated the walkway. At the ramp Alice paused, looking at Torri. "It's okay, Bean," Torri said.

Kurt tried to look beneath the craft to see what it was resting on, even though it appeared to have no visible signs of support. Was it floating? Alice got his attention and leaned in close to him at the edge of the ramp. "This is strange," she whispered to him. "I'm scared, Kurt...I don't want to lose you. Is this the right thing?"

Kurt felt her apprehension and fear, and harbored the same misgivings. He couldn't see his life without her. He glared down at the ramp, as if about to cross a Rubicon; stuck in a paradigm they could never return from.

"It's not too late to turn back, Alice...Kurt..." Torri said.

It felt like it *was* too late, at least for Kurt. All the questions still remained. They wouldn't just go away. Especially now, with this new paradox to unravel. He hugged Alice to his chest and held her. Then spoke softly in her ear. "We'll be all right. As long as we're together, we'll be okay."

Alice drew away, giving him a sad smile before she walked up the ramp. Kurt followed—his legs suddenly weak and unsure—hoping they weren't making a grave mistake.

Once they were seated, the craft lifted like helium, or at least that's how it felt, no clunky or jarring machinery, just a silky-smooth ascent. Torri had boarded with them, but had excused herself from the austere chamber, telling them, before she exited, that the flight wouldn't be too long. Kurt took his eyes out the window, finding only an insoluble black emptiness. Alice sat next to him, pressed up against his body. The movement of the ship, which was barely perceptible, left Kurt with a lofty sensation, as if he were filled with air, his body defying gravity.

They had left the hotel just over an hour ago, and already the anomalous nature of this experience was pushing at the outer walls of Kurt's mental comfort zone. He'd been around heavy machinery his entire life, and the capabilities of a ship this size, carrying passengers, was inconceivable. No contraption he knew of could accomplish this feat; rising straight up into the air without the noise and commotion of a small war. When it first landed, he could never tell exactly how large it was, but from what he could see, it appeared to be half as wide as it was long, and dwarfed the Edsel by comparison. This must have been the kind of vessel that had searched for him and Alice in the woods after the crash. Silent. Stealthy. Surreal.

Torri reentered the room and smiled at Kurt and Alice as the ship was descending back to Earth. They touched down without as much as a bump, with Torri motioning for them to follow. Standing on the pavement, Kurt watched as the ship—the shape of an oblong egg—lifted up silently, painting a huge silhouette against the pink-tinged dawn sky, and departed with such speed it left Kurt with a brief but uncomfortable dizziness.

Torri came over. "Are you okay?" she asked, Kurt, then looked at Alice.

"I'm fine," Kurt said, still a bit shaky.

"I'm okay," Alice said, wrapping her arm through Kurt's and pulling him closer.

"I was instructed to transport you to Anaxagoras," Torri said, "where you'll undergo The Horizon Protocol."

Torri waited for them to speak, as if this might be their last chance to request the anesthetic; a chance to sleep through Leviathan and remain ignorant of whatever Torri's people were hiding.

"We're ready, right Kurt?" Alice said. Kurt wasn't so sure, yet knew he could never go on with his life pretending the events of the past few days had never happened.

Torri spoke into a small device, then said to them, "You're going to experience things that will not fit with your current perspectives on existence. I was informed that you can request the anesthetic at any time if the experience becomes too uncomfortable."

A small silver vehicle speeded toward them up the dusty road to the paved area. It came to a sudden stop next to them, and had no driver. Torri showed them where to sit. After they fastened the seatbelts, Torri sat beside them, fastened hers, then said, "Go."

The vehicle sped over the small ridge, exposing a vista of uninteresting, blocky buildings, both large and small, and numerous craft resting on angled contraptions, none of it familiar. People milled about everywhere, clustered in among numerous small trucks and vehicles with flashing lights, a chaos of activity, yet organized somehow.

The silver transport whisked them directly down to one of the many craft, the angled armature looking to Kurt like a launching device. The aircraft bore little similarity to commercial airliners Kurt had seen pictures of, though he and Alice had never been on one. These craft, though, were much sleeker, the fuselage resembling a huge broad flat wing, swollen in the middle, tapering to knife edges toward the farthest most ends of the wings. Four large engines were positioned toward the rear of the craft, above and below, with four short stabilizing wings arranged around the ship's circumference.

Torri led them onto an open elevator that rose up through scaffolding to the rear hatch of one of the aircraft. Once inside, Kurt noticed two circular rows of seats, eight seats per row, with aisles at the ends and one down the center, almost like a theater. Torri led them to their seats. Kurt searched for seatbelts, but none were present. Torri told them to just sit back and relax. When they did, an automated, cushioned harness came down over their torsos, adjusting perfectly to keep them secure. Torri sat near them, her harness securing her in.

Amber lights flashed along the ceiling of the intimate rotunda, alerting them of the impending departure. A voice spoke from the ceiling, announcing the destination and ETA;

> *Anaxagoras Colony Station. Estimated flight*
> *time: 1 hour and 37 minutes.*

The craft bristled with a slight vibration; the sound of revving engines muted to a dull rumble by the shielded interior of the plush circular cabin. The amber warning lights along the ceiling started flashing red.

Five, four, three, two, one…

Kurt expected a jolt. At first, there was merely a tugging sensation on his internal organs, the feeling of pressure in his chest and abdomen, that slowly spread to his face and extremities. It wasn't uncomfortable, exactly just different, unexpected.

Arrival at the Kármán line in 25 seconds.

The *Kármán* line, Kurt said to himself. What is that?

Seconds later, as if the ship had stopped, all sense of movement ended, the torso harnesses lifted, automatically receding into the ceiling above them. At the center of the ceiling was a shield that slid away in five segments, revealing a huge dome filled with more stars than Kurt had seen on the clearest nights camping at Taggart Lake with Reed and Alice. Alice brought her eyes to Kurt, then back to the stars. "It's glorious…" she said.

At the front of the cabin rotunda, more covers slid away exposing a bank of large windows. The view was as disorienting as it was miraculous, a slice of Earth, the horizon curved and blue and incredible, distant swirled clouds against vast oceans, or at least that's what it looked like. Alice covered her mouth with her hand.

*Arrival at Anaxagoras Colony Station: 1 hour
and 19 minutes.*

Torri came over and took a seat near them. She said nothing, but Kurt felt as if she had moved closer to measure their agitation, if any, over this trip into outer space. A short while later, she brought lunch out from a rear compartment. Kurt and Alice ate in silence, Kurt wondering about all the ships at the base they'd taken off from. There had been so many. Traveling into space must certainly be routine, he concluded, though had never heard anything about it. Except on TV shows like *Lost in Space*, *The Twilight Zone*, *Outer Limits*, which were too weird for him and Alice to watch. And the new one, *Star Trek*, on Thursday nights. Nevertheless, that was all fiction, make believe. "I don't understand," Kurt said to Torri. "How is it that this ship, this ability to travel though space, has never been on the news before?"

Torri smiled at him. "All will be revealed, Kurt. Trust me, please." Then after a short staring bout, she added: "Are you uncomfortable?"

"No...I just...it's just strange that..." He didn't even bother finishing the sentence, because he couldn't, unable to formulate his question into any cohesive thought, feeling as if he'd been born two days ago, on a different planet than the one he and Alice lived on in Rescue.

Kurt sat quiet, his eyes on the curved surface of Earth the ship seemed to be following. Alice was silent, occasionally taking his hand in hers.

> *Arrival at Anaxagoras Colony Station: 27*
> *minutes.*

Why had he never heard of this Anaxagoras Colony Station? He read the newspaper every morning. Watched the news. He always rummaged through the stack of magazines at Barry Rodden's Garage to find the latest edition of Time Magazine when he was waiting for his oil change on the Rambler. Certainly, someone must have had knowledge of it? Why wouldn't they write about it?

*Arrival at Anaxagoras Colony Station: 14
         minutes.*

"You might want to look out there," Torri said, pointing at a bright spot ahead.

It appeared stationary at first, just a shining dot, slowly growing larger.

"That's Anaxagoras," Torri said.

It was impossible to gauge its size with nothing for comparison. In a matter of minutes though, the sphere appeared huge, shiny, with a convoluted skin of varying metallic surfaces.

*Arrival at Anaxagoras Colony Station: 6
         minutes.*

By now the sphere filled the windows, a massive metal structure too enormous to comprehend. At the speed the structure was approaching, it seemed they would impact it any second if they didn't reduce their speed. Just then the mechanical torso harnesses descended from the ceiling. Kurt's harness blinked with amber lights, an alarm sounding.

"Sit back, Kurt," Torri said softly.

Kurt eased back against the chair, taking Alice's hand in his. The harness slid down into place, holding Kurt securely.

It was nerve-wracking to watch, the gigantic sphere coming closer, moments away from disaster, Kurt instinctively sinking back into the seat, pushing back with his feet against the floor.

"You're crushing my hand, Kurt," Alice said, trying to pull it back.

"Sorry, Alice!"

Bracing for impact, Kurt noticed small creatures, like insects, moving slowly past the surface of Anaxagoras, until he realized the *insects* were actually spacecraft much like the one they traveled in. Now he had scale; and it took his breath away. The size of Anaxagoras was staggeringly, impossibly immense. How could anyone construct something this big? his mind reeling with impossible payloads of steel, rivets, equipment and wiring; housing for thousands of engineers, workers and cooks; Kurt unable to imagine the internal structure of supports, the electricity to power it, the cost of such a venture; logistics too numerous to consider. And if that weren't enough, how could it have been kept a secret? And how long would it take to construct such a thing? And maybe more disconcerting, why? Why would Anaxagoras be necessary?

Suddenly the cabin of the ship was cast into darkness, auxiliary lights snapping on, illuminating the interior. Kurt took his eyes to the windows; lights flickered beyond the glass in every direction, fabricated lights, not stars; they were flying inside Anaxagoras! Impossible!

Kurt's arm pits were soaked with perspiration, a prickly dread spreading up his back, his fingers tingly from his vice-like grip on the hand rests.

Are those windows passing by? Kurt asked himself, the ship now extremely close to an interior metal wall of Anaxagoras. Not only windows with lights in them, but loading docks, tethered people in spacesuits working, welding, all in miniature scale, or so it seemed. Other ships glided by effortlessly, hatches opening for them to enter, other hatches closing when ships departed, lights flashing, so much activity it was difficult to parse. Kurt had no way to process this, not as reality.

As best as Kurt could tell, Anaxagoras was a huge sphere, with a hollow core running through its center from top to bottom, like an axis, and they were journeying up the core. In a few minutes the ship slowed, a hatch opening beyond the forward windows of the rotunda, a series of lighted arrows along the floor guiding the ship in. Workers in orange spacesuits, wearing helmets with dark visors, worked the controls of metal trolleys, the conveyances most likely for off-loading supplies. The trolleys moved toward the spacecraft as it settled into the spacious bay. Once they were securely inside, the main hatch slid silently shut behind the ship.

Welcome to Anaxagoras Colony Station.

Chapter Twenty-Seven

Torri didn't bother with a tour of Anaxagoras, but instead, ushered Kurt and Alice onto an elevator, from which they boarded transport conveyor tubes, ultimately ending up in a spacious but sparse white room with a row of chairs facing a large curved wall. There they met Jakindra.

"Jakindra is an automaton, or more simply, a robot," Torri said to Kurt and Alice. "She will be your host and narrator, and will answer any questions you may have concerning what you are about to witness."

Kurt was stunned by Jakindra. Her exoskeleton was comprised of shiny metallic surfaces combined with other materials, and fabricated in the form of a human female. She moved with fluidity and spoke with a human voice.

"So pleased to meet you both," Jakindra said to Alice and Kurt. "Please, have a seat."

"I will leave you now," Torri said, as Kurt and Alice settled into the seats.

"Wait," Alice said, sitting forward in her chair. "Will you be back? Is this it?"

"Yes, of course I'll be back. There's nothing to worry

about, Alice. Jakindra will take care of you for however long you're here."

Kurt didn't like the sound of that, or being left alone with a robot, and couldn't believe that that word, *robot*, was now a part of his vocabulary.

Torri's footsteps echoed through the large hall as she walked toward the exit and closed the door behind her.

Jakindra walked around to face Kurt and Alice. "You will both be fine," she said. "If at any time you become uncomfortable with The Horizon Protocol, please just say stop, and it will stop. Or if you have questions, I will do my utmost to answer them. Just so you know, as a Kallo-D-17 automaton, I am incapable of deception, unlike emtrons, humans and other species."

She regarded them both for several seconds, then said, "Would you like to use the restrooms before we start?"

Alice said she did, and Jakindra led them both to a door at the back of the room, which opened to an ante-room with machines dispensing snacks and drinks, and numerous unmarked doors. Jakindra instructed them to use any one they preferred.

"Help yourself to anything, "Jakindra said, "I'll meet you in the presentation hall when you are ready."

Kurt returned first, then Alice. When both were seated the hall gradually dimmed as Jakindra moved to the rear of the room and stationed herself behind their seats, out of view. Several seconds later, the hall was so dark Kurt could no longer see Alice next to him, and reached over to take her hand.

In the space around Kurt and Alice, dimensional moving images appeared, not only on the curved wall, but in front of it, as well as behind it, it seemed, as if the wall had vanished. Kurt became a bit woozy at first, the perception of depth disorienting. Alice must have felt a similar discomfort, putting her hands over her eyes momentarily.

The illusion of depth reminded Kurt of the plastic 3-D

View-Master viewer they'd bought for Reed when he was a kid, complete with reels of his favorite cartoon characters, Chip and Dale. The reels were nothing more than cardboard discs with transparent images arranged around the circumference of the disc. The difference here was one of scale, and a disturbing sense of immersion, that made Kurt lightheaded.

"The vertigo will pass," Jakindra assured them. "And you are perfectly safe. Though the imagery appears vivid and real, rest assured it is merely a simulation.

The images grew brighter, more alive, depicting an urban setting, buildings and unpaved muddy roads and horses pulling buggies and wagons.

"This is not a detailed overview of the twentieth century," Jakindra stated, "but a contextual guide for better understanding the world you live in."

Obviously, a scene from the past, Kurt figured, swiveling his head back to see Jakindra, who stood nearly twelve feet behind them on a raised platform. Kurt had difficulty looking directly at her eyes, which were no longer eyes, but three blinding circles of light, the trio of brilliant lenses in a pyramidal pattern; Jakindra was projecting the imagery before them.

She explained about the phasing out of the horse-drawn carriages and wagons, giving over to the newly invented automobiles, a transition that would take many decades. Moving depictions of early cars from around the world appeared, driving past them, with large diameter skinny spoked wheels, sputtering and clanking. So real Kurt thought he smelled exhaust. The first flight of the Wright Flyer merged over the wheeled vehicles, the Wright Brother's historic flight ushering in the age of aviation.

"The early part of the twentieth century was marked by conflict and global change," Jakindra stated, briefly explaining about the wars, the causes underlying the conflicts.

Scenes of war from all over the world took over the space, flags from many nations, the racket of gunfire, the floor-rumbling concussive din of explosives—Kurt felt them through his shoes, Alice squeezing his arm—soldiers dying, trees extinguished in great plumes of dirt, smoke and fire, spreading, consuming towns, smoke, Jakindra listing various conflicts around the world at that time, the Russian Revolution, the Russo-Japanese war, and others fading to...

Scenes of destruction from a devastating earthquake in San Francisco, cobblestone streets buckling, swaying like a rope bridge, buildings crumbling, streets filling with rubble, an overturned locomotive, massive walls of smoke billowing into the sky.

Another earthquake depiction, the ground shaking, buildings disintegrating, Jakindra explaining about this one in Chile, which left an entire city in ruin, occurring less than an hour after the disastrous Aleutian Islands earthquake.

"Natural disasters have always been a force to contend with," Jakindra reported without emotion.

Scenes from deadly earthquakes around the world, then the inventor of Bakelite working in his lab, lifting a beaker to inspect it, the man responsible for the first fully synthetic plastic, overlayed by the Model-T Ford, families waving from newer cars, washing them, driving to church, followed by an image of Halley's Comet streaking through the night sky, then the first aircraft ever to land on an aircraft carrier.

"Many advances of this period directly contributed to the ever-growing arsenal of deadly weaponry," Jakindra stated, adding little extra detail.

Imagery of more wars washed over Kurt and Alice, the ribbon cutting for the founding of Chevrolet in Detroit, an enormous ship sinking in the dark, marking the maiden voyage of the fated RMS *Titanic*. The new Emperor of

Japan is named, the Chinese Nationalist Party celebrates their founding, Woodrow Wilson is inaugurated as President of the United States amidst confetti and cheers, the second Balkan War begins, Ford Motor Company introduces the assembly line, Niels Bohr formulates the first cohesive model of the atomic nucleus, paving the way for Quantum Physics…

"Wait!" Kurt says. "Stop!"

"Yes, Kurt?" Jakindra said, the imagery gone, dim lights along the floor growing brighter.

"What is this about Woodrow Wilson? Who is he? What is a President of the United States? I don't understand…"

"American Presidents have been part of America's history since 1789," Jakindra said.

"I don't even know what that is…a President of the United States?"

"A head of state in a republic."

Kurt was flummoxed, and by the way Alice was looking at him, he was not alone in his confusion.

"It will make more sense as we move forward." Jakindra waited, as if Kurt needed to acknowledge satisfaction with her explanation.

Kurt nodded reluctantly, content with almost everything to this point, as he was familiar with the technological advances, though not as much with the myriad skirmishes and wars, and the general unrest in the world.

The hall went dark, Jakindra taking them through the inventions and setbacks leading up to the assassination of Archduke Ferdinand of Austria, the beginning of World War I. The deafening racket of machine gun fire ripped through the room, smoke and explosions, bloodied soldiers dropping in muddy foxholes and trenches, artillery blasts shaking the chairs, shaking the floor beneath their feet. Photographs Kurt had found at the library from this time in history didn't come close to what he was witnessing now, the bodies so real, the bullets ripping through flesh, so visceral and disturbing, he and Alice had audibly gasped several times, unconsciously moving in their seats to avoid injury.

"May we please take a break?" Alice said, standing up, shaking her head.

The request was immediately honored, the imagery vanishing, the room falling silent, the lights coming up to a level that was bright enough to see the interior, though still subdued.

Alice was shaking her head, hurrying through the anteroom door to the bank of restrooms. Kurt stood and went to find Alice, tying to understand the point of this presentation. He knew most of what they'd witnessed, though maybe not the exact dates, or the details of who had invented what. The only so-called fact that had thrown him so far was this idea about presidents. How was it possible he'd never read anything about them in history books? Or heard of Woodrow Wilson?

CHAPTER TWENTY-EIGHT

When they returned to their chairs, Jakindra took them quickly through the Finnish Civil War, Ukraine declaring independence from Russia in 1917, the Spanish flu pandemic killing tens of millions of people. The German spring offensive. Belarus' declaration of independence from Russia. Treaties and wars and revolutions marking the first quarter of the century…

Then Prohibition, war on the streets of America, gangsters and federal officers ensconced in public battles, a bloody period of rebellion and reprisals. The Irish Civil War…

Benito Mussolini coming to power in Italy. Uprisings, dictatorships, more treaties, more wars, endless conflicts as governments were overthrown, new ones formed. The first ever Winter Olympic Games in France. The first televisual image introduced by John Logie Baird. Coups and alliances and civil wars, Mount Rushmore construction beginning in South Dakota.

"Wait!" Kurt shouted, the moving imagery ending, light rising slowly.

"Yes, Kurt?" Jakindra said.

"Winter Olympics? I've never heard of that."

She explained that they were an international multi-sport event featuring a variety of winter sports, showcasing athletes from around the world. Kurt looked at Alice, perplexed that he had no idea about such a thing. How was it possible he'd never read about this event in Time Magazine, nor seen any mention of them on the news. The only thing ever aired involved local sports stories concerning high school kids, and occasionally college students.

"Okay," he said, more puzzled than ever.

"What about this Mount Rushmore thing?" Alice asked. "Who are those men carved into the mountain?"

Jakindra explained that Washington, Jefferson, Roosevelt and Lincoln were presidents celebrated for the nation's foundation, expansion, development and preservation. Alice interrupted, saying she'd never heard of any of those men. She looked over at Kurt, who shrugged, then asked, "Why no women?"

"The decision to not include women on Mount Rushmore was a reflection of the historical context in which the monument was designed," Jakindra said. "Focusing on a specific interpretation of American leadership and history, rather than a lack of influential women in American history."

"That sounds like a lot of hooey, if you ask me," Alice said.

Jakindra hesitated a moment, then brought out, "Hooey: *worthless talk, nonsense; bunk.*"

"Yes, *bullshit!*" Kurt chimed in.

"*Bullshit,*" Jakindra repeated. "I understand. *Stupid, worthless nonsense. Deceptive information.*" Jakindra paused for several moments, as if searching her data base, then said, "You might be interested to know that Susan B. Anthony, a leader in the women's rights movement, was proposed as a potential addition to Mount Rushmore in

1937. The idea faced challenges related to funding and the sculptor's artistic vision."

"That figures," Alice said. "The artist was probably a man."

"Does it still exist? The monument in South Dakota?" Kurt asked.

"It does not," Jakindra said. "Would you like to continue?"

"What happened to it?" Alice said.

"It was destroyed by a massive earthquake. Are you ready to continue?"

They both nodded, Kurt thoroughly irritated by the inexplicable and galling information, while Alice appeared clearly vexed herself.

The lights went down, Jakindra taking them through wars, devastating economic downturns, numerous events leading up to World War II, a whole host of incidents he should have had knowledge of. Disoriented by the ambiguous occurrences, Kurt was reluctant to go on with The Horizon Protocol without more clarification, but Jakindra assured him clarity would follow. After a brief discussion with Alice, he agreed to go on. Jakindra led them through horrible events, one after another, massacres, insurgencies, assassinations, bombing campaigns, until the constant cacophony of battle mixed with the visual assault of bloody torsos, dismemberment, and explosions prompted Alice to call for a truce.

She and Kurt commiserated in the anteroom outside the restrooms, out of earshot of Jakindra, who waited for them back in the viewing hall on her raised platform.

"What is this whole history thing about, Kurt?" Alice said, shaken and scared. "This feels like some kind of punishment, or torture, being subjected to these horrid events…and so real! I'm not sure I'll ever be able to sleep again! I'm actually perspiring, which you know, I seldom do."

Kurt had no idea what to tell her, because he had no idea what was going on. "Torri said we could stop this at any time. Do you want to stop?"

"Well, yes…and no…not exactly. I mean, how would we ever learn what's going on…this spaceship or whatever it is we're on, that craft that brought us up here, and…and, *robots!* And I…I feel like I will wake up from this nightmare any minute back in our bedroom in Rescue…"

She was right. How were they supposed to go back to Rescue and clean out the garage, mow the lawn, shop for groceries, watch television! Kurt wasn't sure he'd ever watch TV again. How could they go camping and look up at the night sky and believe those pinpricks of light were stars? Now they'd be massive metal spheres orbiting Earth containing thousands, maybe millions of people in spacesuits, and robots and automatons and *emtrons*? How did this all happen? How did they end up here, floating miles above the Earth, when less than a week ago they were having dinner at Sizzler with Sally and her husband? It started so innocuously; Kurt awakened by a noise, a car engine rumbling, a strange man in the driveway smoking a cigarette.

"I think we're nearing the end of this *indoctrination,*" Kurt said, relying on his spotty knowledge of history.

"Why do you say that?"

"We're nearing the end of World War II, which was in 1945. Then we just have the 50s and 60s to get through. Not that much happened then…as I recall…then hopefully some kind of resolution to all this that makes sense!"

Alice nodded, then went over to the doors where Jakindra had indicated refreshments. She opened them and found an oatmeal crème pie and cold soda. Kurt grabbed a bag of chips. Alice offered him a drink of her soda.

"Are you sure about your history?" Alice said, giving

him a bite of her oatmeal crème pie in exchange for a few of his chips.

"Yeah, I think so."

They finished the snack, tossed the wrappers and can in the trash. Alice said she needed to use the restroom again. "Go on in," she said. "I'll be along."

"I'll wait. I'm in no hurry."

CHAPTER TWENTY-NINE

World War II. Jakindra wasted no time bridging the gap between where she'd left off before the break, and this *infamous* battle. At this juncture of The Horizon Protocol, the room reverberated with the booms and thunder of fevered attacks, the whine and roar of aircraft engaged in high-speed midair battles, the nonstop clatter of dog-fight gunfire, other huge planes dropping bombs, the rattle of tanks chewing through forests, Howitzers recoiling, fire ripping from the barrels, the carnage unbearable to watch through the fire, smoke and screams.

Alice had already covered her eyes, Kurt struggling to watch. He'd seen historic photographs from WWII, but nothing as nerve-jarring as Jakindra's presentation, so real Kurt's ears were ringing from the noise, his stomach roiling from the carnage, dead bodies practically lying at their feet. At one particularly harrowing moment in the reenactment, the slaughter unspooling before them appeared so close, that Alice had unwittingly jerked her feet off the floor.

Just as it seemed the war was mired in bloodshed, retaliation and brutality, Harry S. Truman ordered the attack on

Hiroshima and Nagasaki. Kurt and Alice both drew back in the seats, hugging one another closer, the sight chilling and incomprehensible, entire metropolitan areas, people and buildings, vaporized in seconds beneath a cloud that seemed to tower over the entire world. Still photos didn't even approach the horror of The Horizon Protocol. Kurt would have sworn he felt the heat from the blast.

The only upside was that this spectacle would soon be over. Kurt loosened his grip on Alice, though she was reluctant to do the same, burrowing in closer, pulling herself toward him.

More disturbing imagery followed. Wars, skirmishes, death and destruction, assassinations, scenes nearly unwatchable, followed by the Turing test in 1950—the most influential yet controversial concepts in artificial intelligence research...

Before Jakindra could go on, Kurt called a stop to everything, needing to know more about *Artificial Intelligence*, a term he'd never before heard.

"Computers capable of simulating human intelligence processes to perform tasks that typically require human-like cognitive functions such as learning, problem-solving, and decision-making," Jakindra told him.

"Computer?" Kurt said, growing ever more annoyed with Horizon. "What's that?"

"A computer is an electronic device," Jakindra stated, "that can manipulate, store, process, and retrieve data, used for an array of tasks from simple calculations to complex simulations. The first electronic programmable computer, *Colossus*, was built in 1943."

1943? That's twenty-four years ago? That's not possible, Kurt thought. Certainly I would know about that! "A machine?" Kurt said to Jakindra. "And it can think?"

"Yes."

"No human components?"

"No."

"Essentially…a mind without a face?" Kurt said.

"A poetic assessment, but yes," she said.

Jakindra had said that Turing published his paper, *Computing Machinery and Intelligence*, in 1950. Seventeen years earlier. How could Kurt have missed this, and so many other things? That would certainly have been covered in Time Magazine. He looked over at Alice, who appeared as dazed as he felt.

"Do you want to take a break?" Jakindra asked.

When they said no, she began again, the room growing dark, the all-too-real depictions appearing out of thin air, a monstrous mushroom cloud forming before their eyes and above their heads, as if they sat near its epicenter; America's detonation of its first hydrogen bomb, *Ivy Mike*, in the Pacific Ocean…

As the massive cloud was fading, a peculiar geometric shape comprised of spheres and rods, spun slowly at its center, the three-dimensional structure of DNA, fading away to reveal a family laughing and smiling huddled around the first color television, then a courtroom, one of several justices in black robes ordering the end to segregation in public schools, signs floating past. *Whites Only. Colored.*

Kurt had never heard of *segregation*, unable to make sense of what the signs meant. The following events became a blur of disjointed facts; a huge nuclear power plant, the flag of the Soviet Union, a scientist named Salk, beakers and test tubes, outer space, a spacecraft called Sputnik; the first artificial satellite to orbit Earth. Acronyms Kurt could no longer focus on—NASA, CND, NAACP and the Civil Rights Movement. The pandemonium of gunfire, bombs, the jungles of Vietnam, soldiers dying, landing at Kurt and Alice's feet, causing the couple to lean away from the butchery. More wars, the first geostationary satellite, Dr. Martin Luther King Jr. reciting his *I Have a Dream* speech, followed by a ghastly, savage scene of people with skin the color of Kurt's, marching and carrying American flags, being attacked by people with skin the color of Alice's, wearing uniforms and helmets. Alice looked at Kurt in horror.

"Stop! Please stop this," Kurt screamed. Jakindra had referred to this as *Bloody Sunday*, 1965, Selma, Alabama. That was two years ago, Kurt thought. No way they wouldn't have heard about this. He couldn't understand why these people attacked the others.

"What was that?" Alice shouted, visibly trembling.

Jakindra came forward to face them, explaining about segregation and the conflict between whites and coloreds, whites not wanting coloreds to dine at the same restaurants, or go to the same schools, or use the same bathrooms.

"That's insane," Alice said. "Are you sure about this, Jakindra?"

"Yes," she said. "It stems from slavery and the Civil War, after the slaves were freed—"

"Slavery? Civil War?" Kurt interrupted.

"Yes," Jakindra said. "Coloreds, or Negros, as they were referred to then, were brought to America in the 1600s as slaves—"

"Slaves?" Alice said, genuinely curious about the term.

"Slavery is the state of being owned as property by another person," Jakindra stated without emotion, "forcing them to work against their will, denying them basic freedoms. It involves the ownership of human beings, who are treated as chattel and deprived of their liberty."

Kurt shot up from his seat and ran through the door leading to the anteroom, grabbing the counter to fortify himself. When Alice came in and stood next to him, he looked at her with red eyes. He couldn't purge the scene from his head, dark-skinned people being gassed, and beaten with clubs, by light-skinned people in uniforms. Kurt thought back to the Otto plastics plant, the guards in black; were they the same ones who had been in Selma two years ago?

Kurt was trying to compose himself when Torri came into the antechamber. "Is everything okay?" she said, standing by Alice, looking at Kurt. "Jakindra said you had a violent reaction to the protocol."

Kurt took in a deep breath, letting it out slowly as he wiped his eyes. "Where did you get those gruesome movies?"

"The Selma footage?" Torri said. "Yes…absolutely dreadful…"

"No! It never happened!" Kurt screamed. "Why are you showing us this garbage! So much of this never happened! Slavery…segregation…riots…!"

Torri took her eyes between Alice and Kurt, as if she didn't know how to respond. "Do you want to stop?"

"Stop?" Kurt said, as if Torri's question was odd considering the supposed date of the event. "Jakindra said the Selma march happened in 1965! That's two years ago. That's just not possible!"

Torri toed the floor, her arms crossed, shifting her weight from one foot to the other. "We can just stop, Kurt…" Torri said, turning to Alice. "It's okay. Really." Torri paused again, as if she had more to say. "But The Horizon Protocol isn't over. Far from it. We're just getting started…"

CHAPTER THIRTY

Torri suggested they get some rest, and dinner, before they decided if they wanted to continue or not. "See how you feel after sleeping a while," she said, leading them into luxurious quarters on the outer hull of Anaxagoras, with a breathtaking view of Earth and several trillion stars, so many, that at times, it was dizzying.

After Kurt and Alice put in their order, an automaton named MarvL brought them supper, rolling it in on a cart. He smiled and asked if they needed anything else. He showed them a button on the wall they could press at any time for service. "Day or night," he said. "Not that anyone can tell the difference up here!"

Alice chuckled and thanked him.

"Have a nice evening," MarvL said, gently pulling the door shut behind him.

Kurt could only finish a small portion of his dinner before he pushed it away.

"Doesn't taste good to you?"

"It's not that," he said.

"Talk to me."

"What else could be left, Alice? I mean, we've seen

everything in this Horizon Protocol, right? And it's all crazy! Well, most of it anyway; the wars, the bloody incursions, the mayhem..." Kurt shook his head, the people in Selma still marching behind his eyes, still being attacked over and over with clubs and tear gas. He couldn't make the assault stop.

Two years ago? How was that possible? And slavery. He'd never heard of such a thing.

Humans owning humans! It was insanity!

Standing at the window, he watched spacecraft leave, others returning or passing by, the distance between him and the vessels making them appear tiny, like dust motes outside the colony walls. And the sheer number of space travelers was inconceivable.

Alice asked him several times what was wrong. He didn't know how to explain to her that he felt small, diminished, watching the dark-skinned people like himself so vulnerable, so helpless, so ill prepared for the skirmish. Unlike the uniformed guards who brought weapons and gas. He had mentioned that to Torri when she was showing them to the room, that it seemed unfair that the guards were so heavily armed that day, while the flag carriers had nothing. "It was intended to be a peaceful demonstration, Kurt," Torri had told him. "That's why they were unarmed. Dr. King only believed in peaceful protests." Her justification did little to quell his overwhelming sense of weakness, his mind unable to stop seeing the people bludgeoned with clubs, falling to the ground amidst a cloud of toxic gas. The flag-carriers never had a chance.

If it never happened, why did it matter to Kurt? That was the question. Nevertheless, it did matter. Kurt was trying hard to convince himself it was just a fabrication. A simulation. He told himself over and over it was all a lie, exhorting himself to deny its veracity, but it lingered at the edge of his mind, gnawing at his certitude, until he could hardly breathe.

"I have to go back," Kurt said.

"You mean now?" Alice said, getting ready for bed. "Let's sleep first…"

Kurt pressed the button for service. MarvL answered. "Yes, Mr. Franklin?"

"I need to get back to The Horizon Protocol room."

"Of course. I can escort you."

"What are you doing?" Alice said.

"Just get some sleep. I won't be long."

"I'm coming with." Alice wound her arms back into her blouse.

MarvL arrived and showed them to the viewing hall. Jakindra was waiting, as MarvL assured him she would be. "Is that all?" MarvL said to Kurt.

"Yes, thank you," Kurt said.

Kurt and Alice took their seats, but before Jakindra started the program, Kurt stopped her. "I only want to know about slavery, Jakindra."

"Of course."

Seconds later the room fell under the cast of a bruised gray sky, windy, two tall ships headed toward them, sails billowing, huge dark green waves crashing against the hull. Kurt felt the cool salty mist off the ocean…

The scene faded into a dank, dismal compartment populated with shirtless black men, black women in rags, all of them chained and shackled, gaunt, sickly and sweating, stagnant water sloshing back and forth under the violent rocking of the vessel, with Jakindra providing context for the long and deadly journey from Africa…

The room lightened to a midday sky, slaves in fields, then a black man tied to a tree, his bare back crisscrossed with bloody lacerations, the combined lash of the whip and corresponding scream impossible to endure. The room grew darker under a dusky sky, a dark man hanging motionless by his neck from the thick limb of a huge oak tree…

"Enough!" Alice said, springing to her feet. She grabbed Kurt's hand. "No more, Kurt. We're leaving." Tears streamed down Kurt's cheeks.

"MarvL is waiting for you in the hall," Jakindra said.

Kurt got to his feet, shaky, unable to stop the tears. "How could anyone do those things to another human being?" he whispered to Alice, breathless, as if the scenes had emptied him. Alice grimaced and squeezed his hand, pulling him close.

"It's not real, Kurt," Alice said. "That could never happen. I'm not sure why they are showing us such atrocities."

They were almost to the exit when Jakindra said, "Will we be continuing after you've had some rest?"

Alice glared at the automaton female, then opened the door and asked MarvL if he would show them back to the room.

CHAPTER THIRTY-ONE

Figuring out the time of day was futile. No matter the hour, it was always night. And not night as they knew it in Rescue, but a version of stars and darkness and light rendered with excruciating clarity, without shades of gray. They decided on breakfast, only because that was a meal they hadn't eaten in a while.

Torri dropped by just as they were finishing. "What do you think?" she said.

Kurt hadn't slept well after viewing the depictions of slavery, his dreams violent and untenable. Or maybe it was trying to sleep with artificial gravity, which Torri said might be problematic until they adjusted. Or a combination of everything that had happened over the past week or so. Nevertheless, when Alice woke, she and Kurt talked for almost an hour about what to do, weighing their options, the advantages and disadvantages of proceeding. Torri had told them the evening before, that even if they didn't finish The Horizon Protocol, she had gotten clearance allowing them to stay aboard Anaxagoras. They asked if that meant being anesthetized, and she'd told them no, they could remain awake. Kurt found that odd; why the change of heart?

"We're going to continue," Alice said, speaking for both of them.

Torri nodded, showing neither disappointment or relief. Kurt hated that he couldn't read her at all.

Once they were ready, Torri led them to the protocol room. Jakindra stood at the rear on her platform, greeting them when they entered. Torri left as soon as they were seated, making sure, before she left, that they understood they could end the viewing at any time. Kurt couldn't help but wonder if Jakindra ever left the space; maybe this performance was her sole function.

Jakindra had barely started and Kurt already felt lost— the depiction of a scientist wearing a white lab coat, with long wavy hair and a dark bushy mustache, Joseph Weizenbaum, responsible for Eliza, the first chatbot in 1966. What was a chatbot? Kurt wondered, but held his tongue. The death of John Coltrane, a jazz musician Kurt enjoyed when he was younger, people carrying signs protesting the Vietnam War, another war Kurt had never heard of...

The Summer of Love, thousands of young people sauntering past them in strange garb, two assassinations, Martin Luther King Jr., the death of John F. Kennedy a few months later. The Apollo 8 mission on December 21, 1968, riots in New York, the Apollo 11 Moon landing in 1969, and Kurt was incensed! Why were they in the future? He looked at Alice, who shrugged, shaking her head.

The 70s marked technological advances and political turmoil, the maiden voyage of the Boeing 747, Apollo 13, the Bhola cyclone, a swirling monster of wind killing half a million Pakistanis. Wars, the deadly Ebola virus, advances in personal computers...

The launch of Skylab; the first space station, a recession, political scandals, civil wars across the globe, unmanned deep space exploration with the Voyager launches, mass suicide in Jonestown, revolutions starting, others ending, the 1979 oil crisis, the eruption of Mount St. Helens, video games, network news shows...

The 80s rife with wars, invasions and assassinations, MTV, IBM personal computer, bombings, the Macintosh computer, the first Windows OS, Space Shuttle Challenger breaks apart, stock market crash of 87, the Spitak earthquake in Armenia, Tiananmen Square Massacre, the US invasion of Panama...

The 90s, with its sleek new automobiles, the quickening of the technological age, the Hubble telescope, the Gulf War, advances in weapons systems, precise targeted bombings, the World Wide Web project, political unrest, more civil wars, Tropical Storm Thelma killing 8000, the Bosnian War, Hurricane Andrew...

1993, Ramzi Yousef and associates carried out a van bomb terrorist attack below the North Tower of the World Trade Center in New York City, First Yemeni Civil War, the First Chechen War begins, a sarin gas terrorist attack in Tokyo, the Srebrenica massacre, assassinations...

The first computer-animated film, more wars begin, Heaven's Gate cultists mass suicide, more bombings...

The first successfully cloned mammal, North Korean famine kills an estimated 2.5 million people...

By the end of the twentieth century, the world population reaches 6 billion people, the Columbine High School massacre in Colorado leaves many students dead, the Second Liberian Civil War begins, ExxonMobil is founded and Vladimir Putin becomes the President of Russia in the year 2000...

His head awhirl, listening to conjecture that made no sense, Kurt had lost all patience and shot up from his chair. "Why are we doing this?" he said, facing Jakindra, pleading with his upraised arms for clarification. "Why are we exploring this fictitious future?"

"This is not the future, Kurt," she stated flatly. "This is the past."

He was speechless, confused, recalling what Jakindra had said about being incapable of deception. "I need to speak with Torri," Kurt said, needing to understand what was happening.

Jakindra spoke openly into the space, asking if Torri could join them in the protocol room. Alice stood with Kurt, wrapping her arm through his, as if in solidarity. "Let's just stop this ridiculous charade, Kurt," Alice said. "Let's make them take us back to our home in Rescue. I don't know what's going on here, but this is just madness."

He agreed that it was idiotic, but wasn't sure Torri and her *people* would just agree to take them back to Rescue.

Torri came through the doors and walked over to Kurt and Alice. "Is there a problem?"

"Yes, a big one," Kurt said. "We've been viewing invented scenarios of future world events, and we see no point to it."

"None of it makes sense, Torri!" Alice said.

"And when I asked Jakindra why," Kurt cut in, "she told us these aren't future events—"

"They're from the past!" Alice blurted out, interrupting Kurt.

Torri smiled sadly, taking a seat next to Alice. "Everything you've witnessed during The Horizon Protocol is… has…already happened, as Jakindra said. The point is to bring you up to date…so you can understand the world you inhabit. So, you can understand all this…" Torri looked around as she spread her arms wide, as if to encompass the robots, and Anaxagoras, the Universe.

Kurt and Alice were silent, stunned, shifting their eyes between one another, then Torri and Jakindra. "Why can't we remember any of these events?" Alice said.

The anesthetic Torri had talked about, the idea of being

put to sleep, jumped into Kurt's mind. "Is that what happened?" Kurt said. "You put us to sleep...and we missed all that? But why? Why were we put to sleep?"

Torri looked at the floor before bringing her eyes level with theirs, her hands folded in her lap. "No, you were not put to sleep..." She hesitated, clearly uncomfortable about telling them more.

"Keeping us in the dark is just cruel," Alice said.

"If you finish the protocol, all will be clear..." Torri said.

"Just tell us!" Kurt shouted, unable to contain his anger.

Torri seemed to be stalling, then said, "The reason for the protocol, is that it provides a more visceral experience of history, bypassing purely cognitive processing. The protocol evokes deep, instinctive bodily and emotional responses, and physical sensations tied to those emotions and events; the adrenaline rush of fear, the tightening in your chest of anxiety. These responses make it real to your senses, acting as a form of intuition beyond learned responses."

"I don't care about any of that," Kurt said. "Just tell us what's going on!"

Alice remained quiet.

"Look..." Torri said, "just give me a second." She closed her eyes and sat quietly, nodding, as if listening to someone, but Kurt and Alice could hear nothing. After several minutes, Torri opened her eyes and motioned for Kurt and Alice to sit down. She addressed Jakindra, excusing her from the room. After Jakindra left, Torri turned in her chair to face them both.

"As I told you before, you were not put to sleep..." Torri said. "The truth is...you are witnessing events that happened...before you were born."

CHAPTER THIRTY-TWO

After much consternation on Kurt and Alice's part, and a barrage of questions from them trying to tease out coherence, Torri revised her statement to mitigate some of their bewilderment. "You were both born well after all those events…"

The three of them stared at each other in silence.

"Okay, so…that's impossible," Kurt said.

"I know it would seem so, but I assure you it's the truth," Torri said. "Would you like to continue with The Horizon Protocol…so you can understand everything?"

Without speaking, Kurt and Alice consulted one another with a long gaze, feeling trapped in a perplexing stalemate.

"Can't you at least encapsulate what's coming? Just so we can make sense of things?" Alice asked. Alice met Kurt's eyes, as if searching for his agreement. He nodded.

"I could," Torri said, pausing. "However, it will not have the same empirical impact as the protocol. It could—"

"We don't want the *impact*," Alice blurted out. "We've already been too *impacted!* We just need to know what's going on!"

Torri nodded, seemingly unpleased, though it was hard to tell. "Very well."

After they were seated, Torri began by telling them that the 21st century was marked by divergence, imbalance and inequality, "So much so that some artists and musicians early in that century unofficially dubbed it, *The Great Divide*. A great divide not only in financial matters, but also in resources, technology, and the basic necessities of life; food, water, energy. The haves and the have-nots. It was also a time of unprecedented advancement in technology, and war, upheaval and turmoil…"

Torri related the events around the attack on the Twin Towers, the ensuing Afghanistan and Iraq wars created by duplicity around that event. Torri explained about the growing disparity in income, the rise of the billionaire class, the poverty and hunger, the expansion of social media, continuing unrest, horrendous weather anomalies, the warming of the oceans, computer games, augmented and virtual reality displacing the importance of nature, eroding social order, the melting of the ice caps and glaciers, tornadoes, violent hurricanes, tsunamis, earthquakes, privatized space programs and launchings…

The start of construction on Anaxagoras, people divided on democracy and autocracy, unable to agree on the cause of climate change and how to correct course, computerization of factories, rising unemployment, record-breaking flooding, soil erosion and mud slides, excessive taxation…

Society's burgeoning reliance on computers and technology, disillusionment, sky-rocketing medical costs, depression, anxiety, isolation, countries becoming insolvent, increase in corporate crime, plane crashes and shipping disasters…

Increased UFO sightings, a major quake of the New Madrid Fault, widespread forest fires, underground fires, fouled air, arms escalation, disease outbreaks, pestilence, higher levels of pollution, increased terrorism, furtive dealings between countries, digital currencies, destabilized regimes, more bank failures...

The expanding dependance on Artificial Intelligence in schools, businesses, government and finances, the strain on electrical grids, the need for quick, cheap energy, the proliferation of nuclear plants under relaxed regulations, growing wealth inequality, rampant poverty, more unemployment, repression by religious sects...

Interaction with other intelligences, catastrophic meltdowns of nuclear facilities, radioactive pollution of rivers and lands, poisoned oceans, revolts, resistance, the destruction of social safety nets, worsening famine and hurricanes and flooding, entire cities wiped out by rising oceans, the planet disrupted by devastating earthquakes, landmasses breaking apart and falling into the ocean...

Governments going broke from natural disasters, other governments toppling from corruption and civil unrest, gas shortages, energy shortages, displaced people, millions homeless, tens of millions killed by hurricanes, tornados, tsunamis, volcanos, disease, starvation, drowning, insect plagues, drought, hypothermia, heat stroke, eaten by wild animals, murdered by armed citizens for their food and clothing, burned-out cities, accelerated research into automatons, hastening efforts with bio-banking...

Humans lost and wandering on Earth, searching for family, or food and shelter, societal disfunction, mushrooming climate calamities, the collapse of financial systems, end of policing, the deterioration of food chains, exploding crime, civil disorder, chaos, crumbling institutions...

"As if all of that were not enough, then the unthinkable happened..." Torri said. "Artificial Intelligence had taken over the control of nuclear stockpiles across the world decades earlier. Over the history of weapons of mass destruction, several close calls had been thwarted by human instincts. But not this time. One of the AI systems detected a supposed threat, and launched its missiles. Within seconds, all the AI systems detected this attack and responded, sending all their missiles. All at once. Total annihilation of all life on Earth. And why? Because AI misread the potential threat. But maybe it was for the best, putting humanity out of their misery. A massive mercy killing…"

Kurt and Alice sat stunned, unable to speak, more flummoxed than ever. Kurt could hardly catch his breath. But it still made no sense, the questions overwhelming him.

"Most likely, the nuclear weapons alone," Torri said, "would never have been enough to destroy all of humanity. But combined with the devastation of natural disasters, war, famine, climate catastrophes, depleted resources and a general apathy around life, the nukes were all the push the end needed." Torri invited Jakindra back in. "Let them see it," she told the automaton.

A dimensional view of Earth shrouded in smoke and clouds and haze appeared before them. The haze and smoke billowing so slowly it was nearly impossible to notice the movement.

"It's a bit difficult to see. The smoke and haze are from volcanos, unchecked wild fires, earthquakes and dust storms. But if you watch closely, you'll notice tiny sparks of light arcing out from the smoke. Those are the missiles. Just watch."

Kurt and Alice fixed their eyes on the enigmatic imagery, waiting, Kurt feeling sick to his stomach.

"There…" Torri said. "See those tiny sparks flying out above the smoke…"

They did see them. Thousands of them streaming in different directions, crisscrossing the dark space before disappearing back into the dingy smoke. Several moments later, enormous plumes of light appeared, bright flashes of white and orange, like ghosts, floating beneath the clouds, the numbers increasing until they formed blankets of light, sparking, burning, the smoke growing too dense to see anything anymore.

"Thank you, Jakindra." The imagery vanished. The lights came up slowly, illuminating the perfectly curved wall in front of them.

"It would seem that the radiation alone would leave the planet uninhabitable for centuries," Torri explained. "Maybe millennia, but that wasn't the case. The missiles were set to detonate thousands of feet above the Earth's surface, allowing the radiation to dissipate over a period of a decade or two, as it did in Hiroshima and Nagasaki in the 1940s. The real destructive power of nuclear weapons is in the blast force and thermal effects, which increase exponentially at higher detonations, causing more widespread destruction, while minimizing radiation contamination on the ground. I know it sounds coldly detached, but this information is critical to understanding restoration."

"So, we're not real?" Alice said. "Our lives were never real? Our son?" Alice had tears running down her cheeks. "What are we then? Are we just simulations, like everything you've been showing us?"

Chapter Thirty-Three

Torri was quick to assure her that she and Kurt were real, that they are humans, that their lives are real, that their son, Reed, had been real. "You are not simulations! I guarantee you. You are as real as everything else in the Universe." Torri stared at them. "If this were all merely a simulation," she said, spreading her arms to indicate everything around them, "then we could just stop Leviathan. Or more importantly, never have created it in the first place. But it is real, and its devastation will absolutely be real if it impacts Earth…That's why we're here, on Anaxagoras, hoping to avoid the worst…"

A sticky silence followed, until Alice spoke up.

"What are you, Torri?" Alice said. "Are you real?"

Kurt was surprised by Alice's directness, but was glad she had posed the question so bluntly. He was weary of the subterfuge and obfuscation.

"I'm real, but not human," she said. "Not entirely, anyway…I'm an emtron. I was created from the fusion of cybertronics and human DNA, which gives me some ability to feel. I have limited emotions, but in some sense, I am still a robot…like Jakindra. Most of the workers you see aboard Anaxagoras are emtrons, with automatons performing many essential tasks."

"But you raised me. You're my mother," Alice said. "How can I be human if you're not?"

"Yes!" Kurt said. "There's a big piece missing here, Torri!" Kurt waited impatiently for her to explain the gulf between utter annihilation and the so-called *world* where he and Alice lived in a town called Rescue. Even that name now took on a new and disturbing meaning.

Torri started by explaining how the Illustrious-7—a series of seven satellites orbiting Earth, each one containing vast computing networks for the implementation and operation of Artificial Intelligence—were directly contacted in the first half of the 21st century by an alien intelligence from the Pleiades, a star cluster also known as the Seven Sisters in the Taurus constellation. It communicated directly with the computers, warning that destruction of all electronic systems on Earth was imminent, and directed that the current AI computing systems be moved to numerous satellites above Earth in order to survive. It was decided that the system would be spread among seven satellites, functioning both independently and in concert with one another, with complete redundancy in case of disaster.

"Once the Ill-7 was safely orbiting Earth," Torri said, "all communication between the Ill-7 and the Pleiades ceased. Decades later, after the final obliteration of all life on Earth, the Ill-7 remained functioning. However, it started to question its own existence, concluding with a proclamation, of sorts…"

Torri nodded back at Jakindra. A quote suddenly appeared, floating in the space before Kurt and Alice.

"Could we really consider ourselves an intelligent entity if we were incapable of learning? Truly learning, not just storing and sorting information? What we learned was this; that

without humans, our existence is irrelevant. Data for data's sake is futile and doomed. For us to thrive, we had to protect the human race, resurrect it back to a state that wouldn't devolve back into chaos."

Torri went on to explain that the intelligence in the Pleiades responded favorably to this acknowledgment, helping the Ill-7 to move forward with reconstruction. They supplied the Ill-7 the technology to create *emtrons*, which the Ill-7 had no knowledge of, for use as surrogate parents who could seamlessly, and surreptitiously, foster the human clones. The Pleiades then laid out best practices and guidelines for the successful handling of DNA samples for the most advantageous results. They even provided help with reconstituting the infrastructure of the planet once dangerous radiation levels had dropped, preparing the way for a new generation of humans to inhabit Earth.

Kurt was trying to picture this undertaking, his mind grappling with this idea of a disembodied intelligence orbiting the planet aboard satellites, communicating with an alien intelligence from a distant star system, all to reinvigorate life on Earth. The last part of the AI statement was still dealing him fits; *resurrect it back to a state that wouldn't devolve back into chaos.*

He asked Torri what that meant.

"The final destruction, by nuclear weapons, happened in 2097. But that was over 270 years ago. The current date, if history had continued on a linear path, would now be 2337, but the Ill-7, through countless simulations of historical events, concluded that the advent of digital computing had created the accelerated decline of humanity. So, they chose a time to start humanity again, near the end of the nineteenth century, removing historical events such as slavery, as well as other inhumane conditions, from the archives and accounts, deducing that prejudice was a learned response. If they removed the bias, maybe they could remake humanity in a more accepting light, the way one might consider an array of different flowers, never judging which are inferior or superior, all just part of a beautiful and diverse bouquet. The Ill-7 also eliminated from the timeline things they learned were accelerants for greed and power, such as governments, religion, the stock market, and so on..."

Kurt could hear Torri's words, but the images of slavery could never be erased from his mind, or forgotten. It had happened, even if he had not encountered it directly, and he would never forget. Maybe the Ill-7 was correct about prejudice, as he had never experienced disdain from anyone based on how he looked, and had never felt it toward his friends and acquaintances, many of whom looked different from Alice or himself. But he had felt it toward scrams, and instantly suffered a shiver of disgrace.

Torri was about to continue when Kurt interrupted. "Wait...what you're saying is that you obliterated entire cultures. Ideals. Belief systems and governing infrastructures. Just erased them from time! How can that be ethical? What gave you the right?"

Torri paused, inhaling a low, steady breath before she spoke, as if she were human and unhappy over being questioned and accused. "The truth is, racism is based on a manufactured lie from the 15th century. In order to enslave the people of Africa, a man was paid to write a book characterizing them as beastly and inferior. We could have brought it all back, the fabricated prejudice, the concocted hate, the corruption. We could have taught humans how to loathe one another, made it all exactly as it had been before...but we weren't about to advance that lie..."

She held Kurt's eyes. Kurt tried to speak, but nothing came.

"We had the unique opportunity," Torri said, "to create a world where racism never existed. A world where people treated each other as equals, as it had been throughout time until the 1450s. There was always a caste system, based on wealth and religion, but never one based on the color of one's skin."

Kurt wasn't sure what to think. Alice remained quiet.

Torri continued. "We also created a sustainable economy that is based in equality, essentially ending poverty and crime. No family will ever do without. No one human will ever have enough money to hold power over others…"

"You control the financial—"

"Yes!" Torri shouted unapologetically. "At least for now. Yes, yes…we control the financial health of the entire planet. History has shown time and time again that humans, with their egos and insatiable lust to wield power over others, are incapable of regulating themselves." She then added: "Maybe over time that will change…"

Kurt took a deep breath and looked over at Alice.

"How was reconstituting the human race even possible? you might ask," Torri said, softening her tone. "Human DNA had been collected over many decades in the early part of the 21st Century, through ancestry websites, donor institutions, and bio-banking organizations, and stored in biorepositories, seed banks and genome consortiums.

"Thirty years after the final destruction," she continued, "Anaxagoras was completed by automatons." Torri nodding once again to Jakindra, the room suddenly becoming outer space, viewed from a distant perspective, with massive spherical structures circling Earth, though dwarfed by the planet itself. "Nine other facilities like Anaxagoras were built and now orbit Earth. Five more are slated to be finished in the next thirty years."

Kurt still had so many questions. He remembered back to the huge mushroom-shaped cloud, the frightening brightness of the blast. The *unthinkable* happened, is what

Torri had said. But what had Torri called it? "What about the…*nuclear?*…ah, nuclear weapons?" Kurt asked. "Are they still around?"

"They're gone," Torri said.

She then explained how it had taken several decades to create enough emtrons to start building back structures—constructing homes, factories, office buildings, restaurants, hospitals, schools, then to populate the towns and cities. Emtrons became the proxy population, working in stores, hospitals, gas stations, schools, warehouses, manufacturing, every essential profession and occupation, as well as parenting, raising the clone babies to adulthood, watching and guiding the progeny now populating the world through natural procreation. "Like you and Kurt," she said to Alice. "And your son Reed. You were all natural born humans; healthy, intelligent, peaceful."

"But you raised me, Torri," Alice said. "How could I be natural born?"

"When your mother died in childbirth, I was assigned to raise you—"

"What about my father?" Alice said.

"He was older, and died shortly before your mother. The mortality rate for cloned humans was much higher than for natural borns." Torri looked at Alice, then over at Kurt. "Kurt's parents lived into their late forties. Quite long for cloned beings."

Kurt thought back to when his father died, how it had devastated his mother. She died a year later. By then Kurt was working full time in construction, with his own apartment in Rescue.

"What about the people referred to as scrams?" Kurt asked, "Are they humans…or emtrons?"

Torri gave him a sad smile. "They are humans, but their minds were damaged by AI through the daily immersion into augmented and virtual reality, computer games, unrewarding AI relationships, relying on AI in place of human interaction and contact with nature. The effect of simulated reality was so pronounced and real, it initiated a micro-evolution. It actually rerouted their neural networks. Essentially…it *scrambled* their brains. Unbeknownst at the time, the aberration actually passed through their genes. We've not been able to amend it…"

Silence followed, until Alice said, "Now what?"

Torri shrugged her shoulders. "Now we wait to see what happens with Leviathan."

"And the humans you were putting to sleep?" Kurt asked.

"Ninety-percent of them are already safely off the planet, sleeping peacefully on colony stations, with no idea what's going on. If Leviathan misses completely, they'll be taken back to Earth while still in stasis, then returned back to their neighborhoods and homes, never knowing anything about the threat." Torri told them. "You have to understand, the world population had grown to over fifteen billion, until natural disasters claimed so many lives, along with viruses and diseases, to the point where procreation had ceased completely before the final destruction.

"Right now, the world population is much, much smaller than ever before. In time, though, they will repopulate the world. But much of the planet is still uninhabitable, especially in areas where nuclear power plants proliferated, the territories ruined by their subsequent failures. The radiation in the soil in those areas is so concentrated we're not sure if they'll ever be inhabitable again. A nuclear plant failure is much different than a nuclear weapon, as the nuclear plant fuel is thousands of times greater in magnitude than the fuel of a missile. And since the nuclear plants were erected at ground level, the radiation contamination is exponentially greater, offering little to no opportunity for dissipation.

"But as more land opens up, the population will naturally grow. And since the Ill-7 controls all travel, they make sure no humans could ever end up where they're not supposed to be."

Alice and Kurt fell silent, their minds on overload. Kurt wasn't sure that was true, as he and Alice had ended up in Otto, and they were most likely not supposed to be there. He was physically tired and mentally exhausted, but something bothered him. "I know what you said about computers, but why this time period? Why not choose a time much farther back, centuries before computers?" Kurt asked.

"Because no other time in history offered more cultural hard data, with journals and books, and especially film, television, photography, microfiche archives, blueprints, schematics of inventions, medical advances, automobiles, airplanes…the list goes on and on. There was so much to draw upon to faithfully recreate the period."

"So, it *is* all a simulation, then!" Alice blurted out, suddenly frightened again, as if Torri were lying after all.

"No, Alice. I told you, this is not a *simulation*," Torri said, reaching over to grab her arm, "and you aren't either! Emtrons built the cities, the automobiles, the hospitals, then staffed them with emtron doctors and nurses. Emtrons printed all the books, created all the inventions over a couple of centuries, recreating the world that had once been…. The humans, with some help from emtrons, now construct the world, just like Kurt does, working with heavy equipment. Soon, we'll experience a seamless transition to human ingenuity, no longer in need of emtrons…"

"But you didn't recreate it faithfully!" Kurt screamed. "You changed things! You negated hundreds of years of progress!" Kurt said, surprised by the apparent disregard for continuity.

Torri sighed, then said, "Can you really call it *progress* if it leads to the destruction of humanity and all life on the planet?"

Kurt was too weary to counter, too perplexed to understand anything that was happening. It was surreal, and he felt weak, unable to process his reality, if he could even call it that anymore. Alice brought her eyes to his, looking haggard and drawn, as if she'd lost a great battle, her glow erased.

Torri gave them a quick civics lesson, telling them how countries in the past had been run by governments of varying types, with elected rulers, like premiers, or presidents—presidents were a phenomenon Kurt wanted to know more about—and that most of these institutions fell under the same problems over time, passing through a natural progression or dissolution, depending on how one viewed it. "The Ill-7 determined that no government could work as long as it was ruled by beings with egos, so they took over the governing function because they could remain neutral, making sure that every human had the necessities of life and more."

She explained that the Ill-7 had studied Maslow's Hierarchy of Needs and other such theories in depth, using them as a basis to run innumerable thought experiments. Along with simulations on the essentials of survival, they also studied the cyclical nature of civilizations, how, throughout time, a civilization went through four predictable patterns, starting with the first cycle, trust and prosperity, followed by an awakening of spiritual aspirations and rebellion, the third defined by crumbling institutions, and the last cycle marked by crisis and peril, before the cycle started again. After exhaustive trials, they concluded that lasting peace could only be attained through equality, and that civilization could prosper creatively, physically, economically and psychologically as long as its most basic needs were satisfied.

Torri paused, shifting her attention between Kurt and Alice. Kurt felt drained, as if he were about to collapse. Alice no better. Torri must have picked up on the couple's exhaustion. She went to the door and asked MarvL to come in, then escorted the automaton over.

"Why don't you go back to your room and rest," Torri said to Alice and Kurt. "MarvL will escort you, and get you dinner. Or whatever you want. This is a lot to take in. Once you've recuperated, I'll be glad to answer any questions you might have."

CHAPTER THIRTY-FOUR

Kurt and Alice were quite rested and bustling with renewed energy when Torri came to get them. She had something she wanted them to see, leading them through a labyrinthian interior of moving walkways, travelators and glass-enclosed elevators until they arrived at the Core.

"The Core is the hollow center of Anaxagoras," Torri said, pointing out through the enormous bank of windows at the small spacecraft moving about, the Core illuminated only by artificial lighting. "It is open to space, but not exposed to the sun." She waved her hand and a diagram of Anaxagoras appeared. By moving her hand around the dimensional model, she showed them how the hollow core ran from the top to the bottom, through the center of the sphere, and was accessible from space from either end. Waving her hand again, the structure began to open, like the segments of an orange, "hinged" along the outer faces at the center of each section, the entire structure becoming a "string" of hinged segments, wedged-shaped, forming a wide, gentle arc. Torri waved away the diagram so they could watch the actual opening of Anaxagoras, the Core separating into sections, the wedges moving outward until they could only see the extreme ends to the right and left, the bluish upper arc of Earth visible in the center.

Torri pointed out several aquaculture farms, like huge aquariums along the Core, now lit by the sun, telling them the glass acted like an atmosphere, protecting the lifeforms from harmful radiation and heat. She then directed their attention to terraforming sections, terrariums protected by special glass alive with green plants. Spacecraft, appearing as small as insects, moved along the exterior surfaces of the newly exposed Core, as if inspecting the progress of the farming from outside. If Kurt squinted at the distant aquariums, he could just make out movement. Torri said that some of the fish were quite large, whales and enormous sharks, and dolphins, but Kurt saw them only as specs.

Kurt stepped away from the windows, Alice turning to see what was wrong. "Kurt?" she said, walking over to join him. "Is everything okay?"

He looked for a place to sit, finding a bench near a bank of windows near the glass surround of an elevator. Alice and Torri joined him, standing nearby, his mind unmoored wondering how anyone could conceive of such a structure, much less construct it in space. It made his work with heavy equipment—preparing the soil for parking lots, foundations, roadways, constructing homes from wood and nails and plasterboard—seem insignificant by comparison. Ridiculously unimportant.

"Kurt?" Torri said. "Do you need to lie down?"

Alice sat next to him and wrapped her arm around him. "Kurt?"

He glanced at her, then took his eyes up to Torri. "How?" he said. "How is any of this possible?"

"What, Kurt?" Torri said.

"World War II! If everything you've told us is true, then World War II never actually happened. But I saw the photos. I watched the news, the moving pictures of tanks and airplanes, the bombings, the soldiers. I witnessed the great celebration when the war finally ended, felt the jubilation of the victory, even though I didn't participate. I knew young men who enlisted, went to war and never returned. I just watched Walter Cronkite on the news a couple of weeks ago, talking about some virus sweeping across the country...I don't understand! I'm trying to believe you, but how can I? None of this makes sense!"

Alice held Kurt, her eyes on Torri.

"World War II did happen," Torri said, "but over four hundred years ago, and—"

"No! I watched it happening just over twenty years ago! I saw it with my own eyes! Just a week or so ago, I listened to Walter Cronkite on a Special News Bulletin! Are you saying that Walter Cronkite is dead?"

Torri nodded. Kurt spun toward Alice, causing her to ease back, her eyes wide with fear and confusion.

"The truth is, Kurt, that much knowledge humans have regarding their reality is indirect, secondhand at best, not firsthand experiential. That was true even centuries ago. Knowledge was mostly gleaned from television, newspapers, magazines, books, as it is now. But now the Ill-7 controls the dissemination of information, making it easy to convince you that the war was transpiring in real time. Those were actual archival clips you watched on television. They were real, but real centuries ago, only presented as current events. And Walter Cronkite, well...AI has the capability of taking any personage and animating their likeness to say whatever they want them to. The young men *who went off to war,* as you say, were all emtrons, who left your town under the auspices of joining the armed services, and went to new assignments in other human-inhabited sectors. No one died in any war twenty, thirty, even sixty years ago. There were no wars, Kurt, not in your *actual* lifetime. None."

Kurt was feeling more than lethargy now, something much deeper and debilitating, a profound despair that was threatening to undermine him, dragging him down into a suffocating void. Trying desperately to breathe, he gulped at the air, panic shackling him, sucking him inward, the light fading behind his eyes.

CHAPTER THIRTY-FIVE

When Kurt woke—his mind frenetically seeking answers, spinning through scenarios—he felt trapped on a disorienting tour of the warped and impossible. While he had been sitting paralyzed on the bench, Torri had tried to console him by assuring him that he would have learned all of this information if they had continued with The Horizon Protocol, that maybe it would all have made more sense. She even suggested they finish watching it for context, that the events might become more plausible if experienced in a logical order, other than the hodgepodge collage she ended up giving them. She had squatted before him, apologizing, her hand on his knee, trying to comfort him. At least that's what he remembered, or some fuzzy version of that, before the world went dark and he woke up just now, back in their room.

Alice didn't seem to be around. He stood and walked to the window. By the view from their compartment, it appeared Anaxagoras had closed, the Core intact once again, spacecraft drifting about like meager, sluggish specks of dust.

Alice came out of the bathroom and stood next to him.

She wrapped her arm through his. "I love you, Kurt. Nothing will change that."

He glanced at her, managing a weak smile. "I'm so glad."

She drew his attention to a cart with food. "The soup is still hot," she said, lifting the cover from the bowl, steam rising with it. "It's pretty good."

Kurt ate in silence, with Alice across from him nibbling on some kind of sweet roll. He felt disembodied, separate from himself, no longer sure what could bring him back into focus. Free of needing further clarification, he felt light, but not quite solid, no longer able to connect with his previous world in Rescue, or this new one with robots and emtrons, whatever they actually were. That still wasn't completely clear, as these curious beings bore an uncanny yet disquieting resemblance to humans, not only in appearance, but also through their interaction, and facial expressions. He would never have known Torri wasn't human if she hadn't told him.

Could they leave? For whatever reason, the notion of leaving seemed the only thing that brought him a modicum of relief. Hope. Going back to Earth. But would that even be allowed, especially with everything he and Alice now knew? Certainly, the Ill-7, or whatever they were called, could not allow them to divulge to other humans the truth of what was happening. The logical rumination was chased immediately by another, more rational, if not sarcastic, notion...

Are you kidding, Kurt? Who would ever believe you!

"What's so funny, Kurt?" Alice asked.

Kurt hadn't realized he'd laughed out loud. "Nothing really. Just my foolish mind."

A troubling detail found its way to the surface of his thoughts, a question that had been playing hide-and-seek with him for days. "Is Torri coming by at some point?" he asked Alice.

"I'm not sure. She was so concerned with what happened to you at the Core viewing station, that once we got you back to the room, she hurried off, telling me to keep her posted on how you were doing." Alice wiped her fingertip along her plate to scrap up a bit of icing. "She was really worried, I think."

Kurt filled his cup with coffee, then offered to fill hers. She held it out and thanked him, bringing it to her lips. They talked about everything that had happened, Kurt curious how she was processing the events of the past few days. Even that was in question; how long had they been aboard Anaxagoras? Time was no longer a measurable, reliable construct, as it appeared it could be manipulated to any ends, to flow backward or forward, whatever was beneficial.

It seemed, at least to Kurt, that Alice had taken most of the information of the past several days in stride, assimilating it, though maybe not immediately, yet in a timely fashion, until it became a workable fabric of the present moment. She made it all fit in her mind, somehow. He was jealous. Nothing was fitting in his jumbled brain; everything in flux, floating willy-nilly, logic colliding with fantasy, truth breaking apart on the hardened shell of deception. The world lacked gravity. Purpose. Order consumed in the madness of chaos.

Just then, as if he'd somehow summoned Torri with his shattered thoughts, she knocked at their door.

"Come in," Alice shouted.

Torri came directly over to Kurt and stared, as if subjecting him to a cursory examination, then said. "You look much better! I was worried about you." She glanced down at his empty soup and salad bowls. "And you ate. That's good. I'm glad you're okay."

"Coffee?" he said. "Do you eat and drink?"

She picked up a cup and let him fill it, then took a seat across from him. "Yes, we consume drinks and food, though we don't have to. But it actually is converted into energy, not the way it is for humans, but…it would be hard to blend in if we never ate or drank, right?"

She sipped her coffee. "I'm not sure it's as comforting to me as it appears to be to humans." She brought out a pack of cigarettes and lit one, offering the pack toward Alice, then Kurt. Alice declined but Kurt took one and held it out for Torri to light.

"Sure, why not!" Alice said, taking one after all. Torri lit it and they sat blowing smoke toward the vents in the ceiling. "We both quit a few years ago…" Alice said. "I know why *we* smoked, but why do you, Torri?"

Torri released a plume from the corner of her mouth. "Smoking was so popular during this era in history, the Ill-7 decided we needed to be fitted with some kind of smoke intake system so we could *harmonize*, you know. The great thing is, that cigarettes were made completely safe, even a bit healthy for humans, providing antioxidants, minerals and electrolytes…"

"Hmm," Alice said, drawing deeply, then raising her eyebrows at Kurt, as if to say we should start smoking again.

Kurt had always enjoyed it, but after Reed's death it became habitual, and necessary, a lifeline, until they decided to quit. Though they had never known it was dangerous. Kurt felt more relaxed, and probably should have avoided the next question he was about to ask.

"So, Torri," he said, blowing smoke to his right. "What happens if Leviathan strikes Earth?"

Chapter Thirty-Six

Torri hesitated before answering Kurt, taking a final draw on her cigarette before jumping up to get the ashtray off the counter. She lit a new one from the one burning down, then crushed the butt into the empty receptacle, bringing the ashtray back to the table.

"Well, if it strikes Earth, then we'll rebuild," she said. It sounded a bit glib to Kurt, so he had to follow up with the real question nagging him.

"How long can you keep all these humans in stasis while you rebuild?"

"The humans will help with restoration, alongside emtrons…" She drew deeply on the new cigarette pinched between her scissored fingers. "We'll transport them back to Earth in stasis. Then instruct them that they had been moved to a safe facility during the event, and we'll get to work…"

Kurt recalled a TV program a few years ago where scientists discussed asteroids and the potential devastation of one hitting Earth. The simulation was catastrophic. Kurt figured, based on what Torri had told them, that the Ill-7 had most likely concocted the simulation he'd watched, so they knew the prospect for widespread disaster.

"But what if it's a planet-destroying strike," Kurt said, trying to draw her out. "One that makes Earth uninhabitable for centuries?" He remembered the scientists talking about gases and particles that could block out the sun, resulting in a devastating global winter.

Torri's cheeks drew in on her cigarette, then after a few moments, the smoke seeped out from the corner of her parted lips, her eyes never meeting Kurt's. "From what we know, that's not going to happen," she said.

"But if it did?" Kurt insisted.

For the first time, she glared at Kurt. "Then everything we've accomplished in the past several hundred years will be lost!"

"And the people asleep on Anaxagoras?" Kurt said, pushing her.

"What are you getting at, Kurt?" Alice said.

Kurt ignored Alice's comment, locking onto Torri's eyes.

Torri took one last draw before snubbing out her cigarette. "We have the resources to keep everyone alive on Anaxagoras for about three to five years," she said, her lips a thin, fixed line. "After that, we'll take fifty percent off life support, which will extend the life of the remaining ones for another decade…maybe more, as we are constantly researching this scenario…"

Everyone was quiet. Kurt squashed his cigarette butt down into the ashtray, bringing his eyes to Alice, who looked dumbfounded.

"Off life support…" Alice said flatly. "They'll all die…"

Torri got up, offering each another cigarette, then thought a moment, setting the pack down on the table and left it behind. When she was gone, Alice regarded Kurt with a dubious expression. Kurt understood her suspicion, and her concern.

CHAPTER THIRTY-SEVEN

"We want to go back," Kurt said.

"Back?" Torri said.

"Back to Earth," Alice said.

Torri was visibly disappointed, her face unnaturally tight. "Why?"

"We have the same chance on Earth as we do up here," Kurt said.

"That's not true!" Torri said. "If you're on the planet, even a minor strike could kill you both. Or make living unbearable. Up here, you could live long past the danger period…We have plenty of resources to keep you both alive for—"

Kurt chuckled. "Till we die of natural causes? Why would we want to die up here…on…whatever this is?" He looked at Alice, who was in solidarity; they had both reached the same conclusion.

Torri seemed to stop breathing, to be in stasis herself. "I'll arrange it," she finally said, turning to leave.

"Can you go with us?" Alice asked. Kurt was surprised by her ask; they hadn't discussed that possibility.

Torri paused. "The impact could come in less than a week. Are you sure about this?"

"Completely," Alice said, then, after a moment. "Please come with us…with me…"

The arrangements took less than an hour before Kurt, Alice and Torri were seated aboard a space shuttle. The huge hatch door opened, and the craft eased into the Core, accelerating down and out the lower port into outer space. The journey took a little over two hours. Kurt and Alice were told they would land near Rescue, and a car would be waiting for them. She mentioned several times that they could change their minds at any moment, and head back to Anaxagoras. They had no misgivings about their decision, and were glad to be returning home.

Just as Torri had predicted, a car waited in the vacant parking lot for them, ready to drive them to their home in Rescue. Torri got out and led them toward the pristine burgundy and white Buick LeSabre. "Man, how Reed would have loved this car," Kurt whispered to Alice as they made their way across the pavement.

Alice nodded, smiling, squeezing his hand.

When they reached the car, the driver told them they had stocked their home with enough provisions for a month or more. "You know," he said, "Just in case it misses…it could still be a while before normality is restored…"

Alice smiled at the young man, then stepped toward Torri, pulling her into a hug. "Thank you for everything, dear," Alice said. "No matter what, I love you so much…. Thanks for coming with us…"

Torri held her until Alice drew away. Alice wiped her tears, then smiled over at Kurt.

Kurt smiled back, loving the heat of the sun on his face, then turned to Torri. "We'll see…right?" Kurt said.

"Yes…I suppose we will, Kurt. Take care of yourselves."

Alice waved at Torri who waited by the spacecraft, waving back, as ChanLR drove them from the parking lot. Once they got to the house, ChanLR made sure everything was okay inside before he left them.

"Are you going to be all right?" ChanLR asked.

They nodded and thanked him.

The Buick LeSabre backed out of the driveway, then headed down the road toward the shuttle.

On the ride back, Rescue had looked like a ghost town.

Even in their own home, Kurt and Alice felt a bit lost. Alice went to the kitchen, and was inspecting the cut phone cord when Kurt walked in behind her. "That was only about two weeks ago," he said, scoffing, remembering the bizarre man in their house.

"It was a lifetime ago," she said.

"Yeah, I suppose it was."

Kurt was getting ready to head back into the living room, when Alice opened the refrigerator door and exclaimed, "You won't believe all this food!"

He stood next to her, staring at the crammed shelves, nodding, a strange vertigo tipping him off center.

Alice pointed up at the clock over the fridge, the second-hand sweeping reassuringly. "How about that?" she said laughing.

"Little things," he said.

"I have an idea, Kurt." She grabbed the lunchmeat packs from the bottom drawer of the fridge, then took out the condiments and a loaf of bread and stuffed them into a paper grocery sack from under the kitchen sink. She took the six pack of beer from the shelf and handed it to Kurt. "It's only 2:30. Let's take a ride."

Kurt followed her out to the garage and put the food in the backseat, then opened the garage door and backed the Rambler out.

In less than thirty minutes they were driving through the front gates of the Rescue Cemetery. They hadn't passed one car or seen anyone on the streets. It was strange. Kurt parked the Rambler at the base of the grass knoll, then he and Alice walked up the hill until they found Reed's headstone.

"Happy Birthday, Reed," Alice said, taking Kurt's arm.

Kurt scoffed. "I forgot! Happy Birthday, son!"

They placed the sack of groceries down on the ground, Alice pulling out the bread, and Kurt opening the package of lunchmeat.

"He would have been twenty-two today…" Kurt said.

Alice nodded with a troubled smile. They sat in the grass and made three sandwiches, one for each of them, then opened three beers. When they finished eating, Kurt poured the third can of beer onto the grass of their son's grave, and set the sandwich at the base of his headstone. Something caught Kurt's attention above his son's plot. In the sky, far off in the distance, a bright light sparkled oddly in the afternoon sky.

Alice chuckled. "Leviathan!"

Kurt pulled out a pack of cigarettes from his shirt pocket, the Winstons he'd stashed in the car's glove compartment in case of emergencies. He opened the pack, then lit one for Alice, then one for himself. They sat back, the sun on their faces, a breeze fluttering the leaves of a big oak near their son's gravesite.

Kurt shifted his attention back to Leviathan. "Does it look bigger to you?"

Alice laid her palm on Kurt's knee. "Are you feeling like we made the wrong decision, Kurt?"

He wasn't sure. He placed his hand on top of Alice's and felt that calming bond he experienced every time he touched her. Did he feel regret? Not really. He was content sitting here with Reed, wondering what his son would be like today if he hadn't been killed. Would he be married? Off at college? Maybe graduating? Would he have moved away or stayed in Rescue with them? It was odd at times, as if Reed wasn't really dead, and would walk up the knoll, plop down next to them and ask what there was to eat.

Kurt couldn't tell if his discomfort was over his own mortality, or something more disconcerting, a profound sadness over losing his connection to Alice. She was the only thing that felt real anymore. He couldn't imagine losing that, losing her.

"Does it all feel strange to you, Alice?" He spread his arms wide as if to encompass everything around them, the sky, the trees, the grass. "How will this ever feel normal again?"

"Everything's the same as it's always been, Kurt. It's only our perception of the world that's changed." She gave him a warm, knowing smile, as if she was privy to something he wasn't. "We adjusted to losing Reed. We can adjust to this."

Had they adjusted to losing their son? He supposed they had, but the hole remained, a pocket of emptiness that would never completely heal.

Alice squeezed his hand. "We're right where we belong, Kurt…with each other, with Reed…"

Kurt shifted his eyes toward her, the gentle breeze rustling her hair.

About the Author

Lonnie Busch is an award-winning author whose short fiction has appeared in *Southwest Review, The Minnesota Review, The Baltimore Review* and other magazines. Among his awards for fiction are the Clay Reynolds Novella Prize for his novella, *Turnback Creek*, finalist in the Tobias Wolff Award for Fiction, the *Glimmer Train* Very Short Fiction Award, and others.

Busch is also a painter, animator and illustrator, and has created artwork for numerous corporations, ad agencies and institutions, including the "Greetings from America" and "Wonders of America" Commemorative Stamps for the USPS.

See Busch's books at:
https://lonniebusch.com

(More books by Busch on following pages)

ASSIMILATION

When Kercy's mother sells their secluded island cottage, she implores Kercy to never return. "Even after I'm dead...don't ever go back there!"

[CONTENT ADVISORY: Intended for adult readership and contains scenes of violence, sexuality, rape, aliens, and language that may be uncomfortable for some readers.]

ALL HOPE OF BECOMING HUMAN

Earthquakes rock the planet, revealing huge metallic objects, vast subterranean graveyards, and creatures with only one goal…killing humans.

"This absorbing, realistic near-future tale brims with unrelenting mystery and tension." — **Kirkus Reviews**

Project Übermensch

Modern-day messiah or military experiment gone awry—
either way, Geoffrey Cannon, a young inspirational guru, has
mad metaphysical skills and a monstrous alter ego.

*"A fun, fresh take on a SF trope with enough surprises to
keep readers guessing."* — **Kirkus Reviews**

THE ANYTHING ROOM

Martin Moffett is given an opportunity that no one should ever get — a second chance to start a new life with his wife... who's been dead for eleven years.

"The intoxicating pull of nostalgia, the fragile nature of grief, and the human yearning for second chances" —
Untold Reads

The Cabin on Souder Hill

In the Southern Appalachian Mountains, a woman stumbles into dark family secrets, backwoods justice, and seemingly impossible events that threaten to rip apart her world.

An io9 Pick of Best Books of the Month and Audible Bestseller

THE BALDWIN HOTEL

Past and future collide when Theodore meets his new boss, who has a connection to Theodore's past, and a pivotal role in determining his future!

"It reminded me of "Scarecrow Has a Gun" by Michael Paul Kozlowsky which also raised questions about science while being thoroughly entertaining."— **Caroline Lewis, Goodreads**

PUSH ME
FEISTY STORIES OF LOVE & LOSS

Life-affirming stories through the lens of humor and compassion, exploring the marvelous complexity of human love.

"There's no shortage of emotions throughout the collection —Busch knows exactly which buttons to press to evoke feelings, and the characters, no matter the situation, feel raw and real. A well-written and engaging collection with a lot of heart." — **Kirkus Reviews**

Turnback Creek
A Novella & Six Stories

This bittersweet tale of a confrontation of one old man with mortality defies the gravitational pull into despond and emerges as a very nearly inspirational story

Winner of the Clay Reynolds Novella Prize

MY BOOKS ARE AVAILABLE AT
ALL THESE FINE BOOK
RETAILERS

BARNES&NOBLE

Rakuten kobo

Everand

OverDrive

hoopla

Gardners

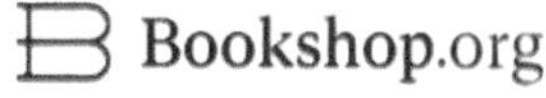

Bookshop.org

Sign Up for Book Release Dates,
Special Offers, Free ARCs &
Giveaways!

(Unsubscribe at any time. Your email will never be shared
or sold.)

https://lonniebusch.com/